TEACHER'S REVENGE

Lissie secretly (or so she thought) unwrapped a piece of grape bubble gum and popped it into her mouth. When Ms. Merriweather wasn't looking, she'd blow a quick bubble and snap it back with a loud click. Her fun didn't last very long.

Once, after the blow and before the snap, Ms. Merriweather turned around and made eye-to-bubble contact. Lissie tried snapping it back fast, but the bubble wouldn't budge. In fact, the harder she sucked in, the bigger the bubble grew.

Lissie stood up next to her desk, her eyes as wide as saucers. She tried to pull the gum from her mouth, but the bubble was now so big that she couldn't even reach her lips. The bubble just kept growing.

There was no telling how big it might have gotten if Ms. Merriweather hadn't clapped her hands and said, "I hate to burst your bubble, dear, but . . ."

There was a loud explosion. Everyone except Lissie dived for the floor, hands covering ears. When the kids looked up, after the blast, Lissie was coated from head to toe with what looked like sticky, purple slime. . . .

Other Bantam Skylark Books you will enjoy
Ask your bookseller for the books you have missed

Boyer

They're Torturing Teachers in Room 104

Jerry Piasecki

A BANTAM SKYLARK BOOK
NEW YORK • TORONTO • LONDON • SYDNEY • AUCKLAND

RL 4, 008–012

THEY'RE TORTURING TEACHERS IN ROOM 104
A Bantam Skylark Book / August 1992

Skylark Books is a registered trademark of Bantam Books,
a division of Bantam Doubleday Dell Publishing Group, Inc.
Registered in U.S. Patent and Trademark Office and elsewhere.

All rights reserved.
Copyright © 1992 by Jerry Piasecki.
Cover art copyright © 1992 by Richard Lauter.
No part of this book may be reproduced or transmitted
in any form or by any means, electronic or mechanical,
including photocopying, recording, or by any information
storage and retrieval system, without permission in
writing from the publisher.
For information address: Bantam Books.

If you purchased this book without a cover you should be aware that
this book is stolen property. It was reported as "unsold and de-
stroyed" to the publisher and neither the author nor the publisher
has received any payment for this "stripped book."

ISBN 0-553-48024-3

Published simultaneously in the United States and Canada

Bantam Books are published by Bantam Books, a division of Bantam
Doubleday Dell Publishing Group, Inc. Its trademark, consisting of
the words "Bantam Books" and the portrayal of a rooster, is Regis-
tered in U.S. Patent and Trademark Office and in other countries.
Marca Registrada. Bantam Books, 666 Fifth Avenue, New York, New
York 10103.

PRINTED IN THE UNITED STATES OF AMERICA
CWO   0   9   8   7   6   5   4   3

To Amanda Piasecki,
without whom this book
never would have happened

And to Wendy Rollin,
without whom this book
never could have happened

They're Torturing Teachers in Room 104

Prologue

There were only seventeen sixth-graders left in Room 104 at Marbledale School. There had been more, but five had been forced to transfer to another school after the taping-the-teacher-to-the-chair episode the first week of the new school year. Of those left, Mitch Baylic, Kelly Wockler, Lissie Adams, and Jerry Sands were the leaders.

No teacher had lasted more than a week in their classroom. Their last teacher, Ms. Pierce, had ended up in the hospital for observation. After a day and a half Mr. Reynolds had actually moved to a deserted island off the coast of Alaska. He wanted to get as far away from Room 104 as possible, preferring the company of polar bears to Mitch, Kelly, and the rest of the kids in the class. The teacher before him walked into the class, took one look at the students, and walked out.

The sixth-graders in Room 104 looked like trouble. That's because the sixth-graders in Room 104 were trouble. That's how they liked it. They were proud of their record, and were determined to uphold it.

CHAPTER ONE

Students . . . 4
Teachers . . . 0

Mitch and Kelly walked down the street. It was early and chilly, and it was a school day, but they were smiling. As far as they were concerned it had been a successful year so far. They were looking forward to welcoming Mrs. Thompson, their fifth new teacher, and they were fully prepared for class.

Mitch was carrying balloons in his right pocket and three bottles of blue ink in his left. Kelly's school bag was stuffed with a funnel and several squirt guns instead of books. "Mitch," she asked as they turned a corner and spotted Lissie and Jerry up ahead, "can I share your books today? I didn't have room for mine in my bag."

"Who needs books?" Mitch said with a laugh. "We're only going to school."

"Oh, yeah." Kelly giggled back. "I forgot."

Mitch and Kelly caught up with Lissie and Jerry. The fearsome foursome walked confidently to Marbledale School. They were looking forward to once again leading their class to victory. They were ready for success. And success was to be theirs that very afternoon.

At precisely three o'clock, in fact, Mrs. Thompson burst from Room 104. "They're monsters! Awful, rotten, creepy little monsters! I quit! Quit! Quit! Quit! Quit! Quit! Quit! Quit!" she yelled. She ran with a limp because one of her high-heeled shoes was missing. But that didn't slow her down as she pushed through the nearest exit door and rushed to her car. Mrs. Thompson's blouse was covered with blue ink, and she appeared to be soaking wet.

Ms. Barbara Franklin, the principal, happened to be in the hall at the time. She didn't try to stop Mrs. Thompson. She knew there was no point to it. "What do I do now?" Ms. Franklin said to herself as she heard Mrs. Thompson's tires squealing out of the parking lot. She also heard Mrs. Thompson laughing hysterically and screaming, "I'm free!"

"I'm not," Ms. Franklin muttered, walking toward Room 104.

As she approached the classroom, she heard the sound of rock music and shouts of "Let's party!" coming from inside. Jerry peeked out the window, which had been partially covered with the pages from a math book.

"Chill, everybody," he whispered loudly. "It's the heat!" All the noise quickly faded amid the sounds of feet shuffling and several *Shhhhhhh*s.

When the principal walked in, each student was seated at his or her desk, hands folded and smiling. "Good afternoon, Ms. Franklin," Kelly cooed like a pigeon.

"You did it again, didn't you?"

Jerry raised his hand. "Did what, Ms. Franklin?" he asked sweetly.

Ms. Franklin looked at the empty squirt guns, the partially flooded floor, and the remains of an ink-filled balloon on the teacher's chair. She folded her arms. "Okay. What happened?"

The class also looked at the squirt guns, the floor, and the teacher's ink-stained chair. Lissie shrugged

5

her shoulders. "Nothing." Giggles filled the room. Jerry was out-and-out laughing.

Ms. Franklin's hands began to tremble. Her face started to turn red. Her lower lip was quivering, and then . . . the bell rang.

"Have a nice day, Ms. Franklin," Mitch said, walking up to the principal and shaking her hand as all the other kids started to file out.

"What do I do now?" Ms. Franklin repeated again and again on her way back to her office. There wasn't a teacher in the district who would take on Room 104. Maybe not even one on the whole planet. By the time she reached her office, only one word kept going through her mind: "HELP!"

The school secretary stopped Ms. Franklin before she could open her office door. "Excuse me, Ms. Franklin, but there's someone waiting in your office to see you."

"Don't tell me. It's the FBI. Room 104 finally made it onto the ten least wanted list."

"No. She gave me this." The secretary handed Ms. Franklin a business card.

Rebecca Merriweather—Teacher

Ms. Franklin looked at the school secretary and raised one eyebrow.

"She said you'd be expecting her," the secretary told her. "I think I should warn you that Ms. Merriweather seems a bit strange."

"A bit strange?"

"Yes. When I asked why she wanted to see you, she said you asked for ... "

"Asked for what?"

"Help."

Rebecca Merriweather sat quietly in the principal's office. She smiled as she read a book at an incredible speed. Page 1, 3, 5, 17, 30, 52, 76 ... the pages flew by in a blur. When Ms. Franklin walked in, Rebecca Merriweather finished the last page (277) and put the book into her green cloth bag with the blue tie around the top.

Ms. Franklin stopped in her tracks. Ms. Merriweather was indeed a rather strange sight. Her shoulder-length hair was so blond that it was closer to white. Her skin was smooth and without makeup, and her big blue eyes sparkled like a child's on Christmas morning. And yet Ms. Franklin felt that

Ms. Merriweather was much older than she appeared ... much, much older.

Ms. Merriweather's clothing was more than a bit unusual for a teacher. In fact, she looked more like a student who had gotten dressed in a big hurry, and in the dark. She wore a long, almost knee-length, purple knit vest with pockets everywhere. Under that was a turquoise turtleneck with yellow stripes. The floor-length patterned skirt she wore was gold, silver, plum, and peach. She had on red, high-top sneakers. On her head rested a purple beret.

Ms. Merriweather rose and extended her small hand to Ms. Franklin. The principal took her hand slowly. She was shocked to find that, standing up, Ms. Merriweather was just about the size of most of the students in the sixth grade.

"You know what they say about good things coming in small packages," Ms. Merriweather said, as if reading Ms. Franklin's mind. "And yes, I do think it would be a good idea if you sat down."

"I was just thinking that," Ms. Franklin said as she moved to her desk and took a seat. "What can I do for you Ms. ... ahh ... Ms. ... ahh ... "

"Merriweather. But you can call me Rebecca." Ms. Merriweather smiled a radiant smile.

Ms. Franklin cleared her throat. "I'm sorry if I seem a bit confused, Ms. Merriweather. But I was rather startled to find you in my office. I really wasn't expecting you, and—"

"Of course you were, my dear," Ms. Merriweather gently interrupted. "We have an appointment."

Ms. Franklin didn't remember any appointment, but decided against discussing it any further. "Well, you're here, and I'm here. So how can I help you?"

"I'm here to apply for the teaching position," Ms. Merriweather replied matter-of-factly.

"Teaching position?"

"I do believe you have one open."

"How did you know about that?"

"Would you believe a little birdy told me?"

For a moment Ms. Franklin thought that she heard a little bird twittering. *Nah*, she thought. Now I'm hearing things.

"Sometimes when we're hearing things, it's wise to listen." Those words just popped into Ms. Franklin's mind. She thought she heard a voice in her head. It sounded sort of like Ms. Merriweather's voice . . .

"Ms. Franklin. Ms. Franklin." The principal was

jerked back to reality by Ms. Merriweather's voice. This time it came from Ms. Merriweather.

"I'm sorry," Ms. Franklin said. "I must have been daydreaming."

"Some of my best dreams come during the day," Ms. Merriweather told her, smiling. "But let's get down to business. I have much to do before class tomorrow."

"Ms. Merriweather, I cannot just hire a teacher off the street."

"Piddle-dee diddle-dee. Of course you can hire me. You're the principal."

"No, I can't. And excuse my bluntness, Ms. Merriweather, but I don't even know you."

"Are you sure?"

Ms. Franklin was about to say that of course she was sure, but she didn't. There was something familiar about Ms. Merriweather, but what? The principal returned to the facts at hand, determined to talk about why she just couldn't hand out jobs as if they were Halloween candy. Instead she looked into Ms. Merriweather's eyes, paused for a moment, and before she could stop herself said, "You're hired."

"Thank you, my dear," Ms. Merriweather said.

10

She stood up, shook hands, and headed for the office door.

"Wait," Ms. Franklin called. "You don't even know what room to report to."

"Room 104, right?" Ms. Merriweather said as she dashed out of the office. "See you tomorrow."

"What did I do?" Ms. Franklin wondered out loud. She got up and ran after Ms. Merriweather. "Wait. Ms. Merriweather, wait." The newly hired teacher had only a few steps' head start on the principal, but when Ms. Franklin came out of the office, Ms. Merriweather was gone. "Where did she go?" Ms. Franklin asked her secretary.

"Who?"

"Ms. Merriweather."

"Isn't she still in your office? I didn't see her leave."

"You must have seen her."

"Nope."

"Well, then you must have gone for coffee or something."

The secretary looked at the empty, dry coffee cup next to her typewriter and shook her head.

Ms. Franklin walked back into her office and found her calendar. Under today's date she read:

"Mr. and Mrs. Fredrickson—10:30 A.M. Teachers meeting—12:30 P.M. Fire drill—2 P.M. Ms. Merriweather—3:30 P.M." All of the appointments were written in her own handwriting. The only difference between them was that all but the last had been written in black ink. That one was in purple . . . and the ink wasn't completely dry.

CHAPTER TWO

Introducing Sidney

At 8:45 the next morning the students of Room 104 stood in line at the front door of Marbledale School. Mitch shifted his weight from one foot to the other. Kelly kept looking at her new watch in a way that made sure everyone else saw it, too. Lissie held her school bag tightly in one hand while reading a *Betty's Diary* comic book. Jerry chanted, "New meat, new meat" softly to himself. Like overeager boxers waiting for a championship bout, they waited for the bell to ring. They just had to find out who would be brave or foolish enough to take the 104 challenge.

"Whatcha got, Lissie?" Mitch asked out of the side of his mouth.

Lissie had volunteered to bring most of the supplies they needed for class that day. "I didn't have much time," she said. "I just brought some of the old faithfuls." Lissie pulled out a tube of Super Glue for gluing the teacher's books shut, a leaky fountain pen, a small saw for shortening one leg of the teacher's chair, a tack for her seat, some raspberry Jell-O for her coat pocket, finger paints, vampire fangs, a rotten tomato, and a good supply of very shootable rubber bands.

"Not bad for starters," Mitch said as he inspected the arsenal.

While Mitch, Lissie, and the rest planned their teacher-toppling strategy, Ms. Franklin arrived at work. She hadn't slept very well the night before. She kept having a strange dream. She dreamed she was twelve years old again, sitting at a desk in the first row of a classroom filled with sixth-graders. She looked around at all her classmates.

"Barbara, you simply must start paying more attention in class," a voice from the front of the room said. Ms. Barbara Franklin turned around to see a smiling Ms. Merriweather. She raised her hand to ask Ms. Merriweather a question, but then woke up.

It happened all night long. But now Ms. Franklin was wide awake. This time she was going to ask her questions and get some answers from good old Ms. Merriweather.

Mitch and Lissie had gathered their friends into a huddle. Lissie was passing out rubber bands to everyone. "When I say good morning to the new teacher, start shooting," she instructed.

Mitch walked around like a football coach on the day of a big game. "Okay, team," he said in a strong voice. "Yesterday was good, but I want today to be even better. I want a record this time."

"Yeah," Lissie agreed. "Let's see if we can get rid of this one before we go to lunch. I need to go to the mall this afternoon."

"That's gives us"— Kelly flashed her new watch—"three hours and twenty-two minutes."

"Can we do it?" Mitch yelled.

"Yeah!" everyone yelled back.

"I can't hear you," Mitch shouted.

"YEAH!" they screamed as the bell rang.

"Well, then let's get in there and get the job done

the way only we can!'' Everyone slapped high fives and headed for the door.

As they marched into the school building, Jerry led them in the official Room 104 fight song:

> The teacher is no dreamboat,
> she really has a smell (PU),
> she's rotten and she's stinky,
> and she can go to . . .
> Hello, operator,
> we're really feeling fine,
> and if we see our teacher,
> we'll kick her fat . . .
> Behind the refrigerator,
> she's looking for our class.
> We've oiled up the floor
> so she'll fall right on her . . .
> Ask us no more questions,
> not another word.
> We won't give any answers
> because our teacher is a nerd.

Meanwhile Ms. Franklin had taken her search for answers right to the source of her questions. But when she opened the door to Room 104, she immediately forgot everything she'd planned to say. The room was completely empty, except of course for Ms. Merriweather. She was busily dusting the windowsills with a bright yellow feather duster. "Good morning, my dear," Ms. Merriweather sang as she continued her work. "A beautiful day, don't you think?"

"Ms. Merriweather . . . " Ms. Franklin began in a rather panicky voice. "The bell's going to ring any second now."

Ms. Merriweather pulled a large gold pocket watch out of her vest. "I'd say in about twelve-point-eight seconds from right now."

"But there are no desks . . . no books . . . not even a blackboard."

"Piddle-dee diddle-dee. You worry so much. I expect my materials to be here in plenty of time," replied the teacher.

The bell rang. Ms. Merriweather looked at her watch and shook her head. "One-point-two seconds slow. I must get this fixed." She put the watch back in her vest pocket. Ms. Merriweather took Ms. Franklin by the arm and led her toward the door. "Now, not to worry, dear. You just go and take care of your principaling, and leave Room 104 to me."

"But, Ms. Merri—"

"No buts, no ifs, no ands. And no questions." Ms. Merriweather shooed Ms. Franklin out the door, closing it behind the principal with a quick "Ta ta."

Ms. Franklin heard the door lock. That's odd, she thought. That lock hasn't worked in years.

As they walked down the hall, Mitch was ready, Lissie was ready, Jerry was ready, and Kelly kept looking into every classroom window at her reflection to make sure her hair was ready. But in the end they weren't at all ready for what they found in Room 104.

"Hey, where are our desks?"

"Where are the chairs?"

"Where's the blackboard?"

"Where's the teacher?"

The room was completely empty. Well . . . almost. At the front of the room was a large box. It was dark red with the words "Do not touch. Do not kick. Do not stomp. Do not tease. Do not pound. And if I were you, I wouldn't even look!" written on it in large blue letters. The box was about seven feet long and four feet wide, and only three or four inches thick.

"What on earth is that?" Mitch asked no one in particular.

"Maybe it's a mirror," Kelly said in an excited voice as she fluffed out her hair with her hands.

Ms. Franklin had just returned to her office, more confused than ever. She looked into a mirror that hung behind her door. "Okay, kid, what do you do now?" she asked her reflection.

With all the unusual things that had happened over the past twenty-four hours, Ms. Franklin half expected her reflection to answer her. But it just stared silently back at her.

In Room 104 everyone began to guess what was in the box. Everyone had an opinion. Everyone was wrong.

"Maybe it's a basketball backboard," Mitch suggested.

"No way," Kelly replied. "It's too long."

"I bet there's nothing in that old box at all," Lissie said. Her eyes narrowed. "I bet it's just some teacher-type trick to mess up our plans."

"Only one way to find out," Jerry declared as he started walking toward the box.

"Don't come any closer, turtle-breath."

"Who said that?" Jerry stopped in his tracks and looked at his classmates, who just shrugged their shoulders.

"Said what?" Mitch asked.

Jerry hesitated. He looked at the box and then back at his friends. It no longer seemed like such a good idea to look into the box. "Who cares about a stupid teacher's box, anyway?" He started to turn around.

"What's the matter?" a boy named Ian asked. "You chicken?"

"I ain't chicken of nothing," Jerry snarled.

"Then go see what's in the box," Ian challenged.

The whole class joined in. "Yeah." "Go on." "Chicken." "Buc-buc-buc. Buc-buc-buc."

"Shut up," Jerry snapped, moving toward the box again.

"Bad choice, Jer." He heard the voice once more, but this time he kept walking. No one was going to call Jerry Sands chicken. He was five steps from the box, then four, two, and one. He suddenly stopped. His feet wouldn't budge.

"He is a chicken," Ian exclaimed with a laugh.

"Shut up, jerk-face. I can't move. Look," Jerry said.

Jerry tried to lift his shoes, but could move them only half an inch off the floor before they were pulled back down by black, gooey tar. "Help me, you guys," he called.

Mitch ran over and pulled Jerry's arms. His hand stuck fast to Jerry's shirt. "I can't let go," Mitch yelled. Ian grabbed Mitch around the waist and pulled, only to find himself stuck to Mitch's pants. Lissie and another girl took hold of Ian's legs and instantly stuck. All the others, except for Kelly, tried to help, only to find themselves attached to the people in front of them. It looked like a long train, except the sixteen boxcars were alive and screaming for help.

Kelly was the only one still free. "You all look sooo ridiculous," she said with a giggle. "It's just a dumb old box." She walked over and confidently placed her hands on the box. "See. I told you."

"*Oh, yeah?*" Those words were the last thing Kelly heard before a loud clap of thunder rocked the room. Flashes of light streaked up her arms. Her whole body seemed to sparkle and shake. She looked like Fourth of July fireworks. Then there was a crackling sound, and a thousand tiny lights glimmered around her head. When they vanished, Kelly's hair stood straight up. "Oh, noooo!" she shrieked. "It frizzed my hair."

"Forget your dumb hair!" Jerry cried. "Get us out of here!"

"My hair. My beautiful hair." Kelly slumped down in a corner and touched her hair, which now resembled a Halloween wig.

Mitch decided to take charge. "Okay," he yelled. "On the count of three we all pull. Ready? One, two, three!"

Everyone pulled and pulled and pulled. Nothing and no one moved. In fact, the harder the kids pulled, the more they seemed to be stuck. All of them were groaning and straining their muscles, trying to break free. They were getting nowhere until they heard a woman's voice say, "Sidney! Stop that this instant!"

As soon as they heard those words, the students found themselves flying backward at full speed. It was as if someone had taken off a powerful brake, or had let go of a rope during a tug-of-war. They all landed in a pile at the back of the room.

"Hello, class. I'm Ms. Merriweather, your new

teacher. And from the looks of things, you could certainly use one." Everyone looked up from the pile.

"Good morning, Ms. Merriweather," Lissie moaned. No one shot a rubber band.

All at once the kids thought they heard a happy whistling sound coming from inside the box. Apparently Ms. Merriweather heard it, too. She walked up to the box, folded her arms, and said, "Very naughty, Sidney. Very naughty indeed." The whistling faded. Ms. Merriweather turned back to the class. "Now, who would like to help me unload Sidney?"

"Don't touch that thing!" the whole class screamed at once.

"Nonsense." Ms. Merriweather started to open the box. The students all held their breath. Nothing happened.

"You see," Ms. Merriweather explained as she lifted the top off the box. "You just have to know what you're getting into before you get into it."

Ms. Merriweather looked over at Kelly, who was still in the corner and as white as a ghost. "Kelly, dear," she said, "what ever happened to your hair?"

CHAPTER THREE

Opportunity Knocks

Unaware of the sticky and hair-raising events that were taking place in Room 104, Ms. Franklin had decided to track down some facts about Ms. Merriweather. But what Ms. Franklin found was nothing.

The local teachers union had no record of an R. Merriweather. Neither did the state education association or even a national teachers group in Washington, D.C. Ms. Franklin had found a Merriman, a Merriter, a Merrywells, and two Merrivilles, but no Merriweathers.

Ms. Franklin leaned back in her chair and rubbed her forehead. She felt a headache coming on.

In Room 104 Ms. Merriweather pulled a tiny plastic tab on the side of the box and opened it like a pack of gum. As the cardboard fell away, the class ducked down, expecting the worst. Jerry threw himself on to the floor and screamed, "Incoming!"

"I would like you all to meet Sidney," Ms. Merriweather said. "He's my teaching assistant."

No one looked up. Mitch thought that Sidney was going to be a slithery, slimy monster. Lissie thought Sidney would be some sort of child-chomping machine. Jerry pictured Freddy Krueger, and Kelly envisioned a punk hairdresser with razor blade earrings.

"Come, come, class. We mustn't be afraid of silly Sidney," Ms. Merriweather said. "I'm sure he'll want to behave himself from now on."

When the students finally lifted their fingers from their eyes, they didn't see a monster, a machine, a maniac, or a madman barber. What they saw was a door. It was even a rather ordinary door at that. It was white, and some of the paint was peeling. It had a tarnished brass knocker and a gray doorknob. It stood in a plain white wooden frame. A dull gray metal nameplate was mounted on the top board of the frame. Kelly noticed that part of the *y* in the name Sidney had been worn away.

Ms. Merriweather lifted the brass knocker and banged it three times. Lissie swore she heard a voice say, "Come in." But then again, she might have imagined it.

After the third knock Ms. Merriweather said, "I do believe that was opportunity knocking. I'm quite sure of it." Ms. Merriweather knocked three times more. "Yes, indeed. You all now have an opportunity to actually learn something in school, and to show everyone that the students in this class are not the diddle-dee-dups that everyone thinks they are." Ms. Merriweather walked slowly toward the back of the classroom. "Anyone interested in answering the call and opening the door?" She spun around and looked directly at Kelly.

"Kelly, how about you? Will you open Sidney? Will you take a chance?"

Kelly moved even farther into the corner. How did Ms. Merriweather know my name? she wondered. "No way. No how. Na uh. Forget it!"

26

"Kelly," Ms. Merriweather said in a soothing voice. "Sometimes we must do . . . in order to undo. She looked up at Kelly's hair meaningfully. Open the door."

"No."

"Kelly?"

"No."

"Kelly!"

"No."

Ms. Merriweather looked deep into the girl's eyes. "Open the door. Now, Kelly." Kelly heard the words clearly, but Ms. Merriweather hadn't moved her lips. She tried to look away, but couldn't. Kelly knew that she was not about to open that door. Nonetheless, she found herself getting up and walking toward it. Kelly never lost eye contact with Ms. Merriweather.

"Don't do it, Kell!" Mitch yelled.

The rest of the class joined in. "Don't, Kelly!" "Stop!" "Don't fall for it!" "Stop, Kelly, stop!"

"*Now*, Kelly." Ms. Merriweather's eyes looked soft and caring. Kelly reached out and touched the doorknob.

"You jerk!" Jerry screamed.

Again the rest of the class chimed in. "Stop,

27

turkey." "Traitor." "Teacher lover!" "Geek!" "Yeah, Kelly's a geek!" "Geek!" "Geek!" "Geek!" "Geek!"

Kelly barely heard the shouts of her classmates. She opened the door. There was a sudden gust of wind that grew into a gale. The whole class, except for Kelly, was blown backward against the wall. One might have thought the screams from Room 104 could be heard a mile away. But the custodian, who was walking by at the time, heard nothing.

While her classmates fought to peel themselves from the wall, Kelly stood calmly in front of the open door. "You can close it now, Kelly," she heard Ms. Merriweather whisper in the wind.

Without a word Kelly closed the door. The wind stopped, and the students slumped to the floor. Ms. Merriweather handed Kelly a mirror. Her hair was now perfect. In fact, it was better than perfect. It even had a new red ribbon tied in a bow. "See, Kelly," Ms. Merriweather said, smiling. "When opportunity knocks, it's a good idea to answer."

Kelly smiled from ear to ear as she turned toward her friends. Then she started to laugh. Ms. Merriweather laughed, too.

"What are you two laughing at?" Jerry demanded from the bottom of the pile of students. Kelly and

Ms. Merriweather were now laughing too hard to answer.

Every student's hair had been blown straight up on end, making the kids look like cartoon characters who had stuck their fingers into electric sockets. Ms. Merriweather shook her head and giggled. "I should have warned you, class. Sidney hates the word *geek*."

The class stood in stunned silence as Ms. Merriweather regained her composure. Kelly, however, couldn't contain herself.

The sight of her friends with electric hair was one of the funniest things she'd seen since Roseann Collins had written a dirty word on her arm and then been unable to get it off for a week.

She kept laughing, until she saw Jerry. He was staring at her. There was absolutely no amusement in his look at all. Kelly tried to cover her laughing by coughing. "Excuse me, Ms. Merriweather. May I get a drink of water?" Kelly coughed.

"I think that would be a good idea, Kelly."

As soon as Kelly left the room and closed the door, her coughing turned once again to hysterical laughter.

"Okay, my frizzettes, shall we get to work?" Ms.

Merriweather asked pleasantly. "First things first. I want you all to turn around three times with your eyes shut. No peeking."

"Why should we listen to you?" Jerry sort of snarled.

"Do you want to look like something out of shock theater forever? If we don't do something within the next"—Ms. Merriweather pulled her watch out of a vest pocket—"thirty-two seconds, your new hairdos will become permanent."

"Oh, yeah, sure. Tell us another one," Jerry replied, smirking.

"Shut up, Jerry," Lissie whispered. "We better do what she says . . . for now."

The students closed their eyes and started to turn.

"Remember, no peeking," Ms. Merriweather warned.

They turned once . . . twice . . . three times. On turn three Lissie stumbled, banged her shins into something hard, and cried, "Ouch." With that the kids opened their eyes. They were quite surprised by what they saw.

Their hair now back to normal, the students were standing next to shining, pure white desks. New blackboards sparkled on the front wall. Hanging from the ceiling in one corner was a three-foot crystal globe. In another corner hung a model of the starship *Enterprise*. Something was funny, though—no one could see any strings holding them up. The walls, which had been bare, were now covered with posters, maps, and pictures.

But the strangest thing of all was the six-foot thermometer that now stood behind Ms. Merriweather's huge antique desk. Instead of degrees the thermometer had the words *cool, warm, annoyed, angry,* and *I can't be responsible for what I might do now* written on it from bottom to top.

"Where did all this come from?" Mitch asked.

"The world can change in the blink of an eye, Mitchell," Ms. Merriweather said. "Besides, just because you couldn't see it before doesn't mean it wasn't here all along." Ms. Merriweather's comments were cut short by snickering in the back row.

Everyone turned, looked, and laughed. Everyone, that is, except the person the whole class was now looking and laughing at. Some pointed fingers. Some put their hands over their mouths to muffle their laughter. Some, like Mitch, started banging on their new desks while making grunting noises.

"Hey, what's going on?" Jerry demanded. "You guys better not be laughing at me."

"Maybe you should learn to laugh at yourself," Ms. Merriweather said as she pulled a hand mirror out of a vest pocket and placed it on Jerry's desk. Jerry picked it up, looked, and screamed.

Jerry's hair, which had been straight, was now a mass of tight pin curls, fluffed up on top . . . and held in place with a pale pink bow. And . . . his hair was blue.

Ms. Merriweather shrugged her shoulders. "I told you not to peek."

CHAPTER FOUR

Finius Q. Sands
to the Rescue

After school that day Jerry raced home with his school bag over his head. He didn't take it off until he opened his front door. Jerry had barely walked into his house when he was confronted by his father. When Jerry's father saw Jerry's blue hair, his face turned beet red. "You have blue hair! How dare you have blue hair?"

"Hello, Father. Nice to see you, too," Jerry replied sarcastically.

"You have blue hair!"

"I know, Dad. I know."

Jerry's father started pacing back and forth. "No son of mine is going to be walking around town with blue hair. I have a reputation to think about. No one in my family has ever had blue hair."

"I know, Dad. I know," Jerry repeated.

"Do you think I have even a teeny-tiny chance of being reelected to the school board if it gets out that my son has blue hair? Why did you do it to me, Jerry? Why? Is it some kind of runk pock thing?"

"That's punk rock, Dad." When Jerry's father became upset, he tended to reverse the first letters of words. It drove Jerry's mom crazy.

"Next you'll want a safety pin through your nose, and have your ears pierced with a fork so you can get four earrings in," Jerry's father spluttered.

"Dad, I didn't make my hair blue."

"Sure. I bet some blue-haired fairy godmother just wiggled her wand and—poof!—your hair was blue."

"Ms. Merriweather did it, Dad."

"Who is she?"

"My new teacher," Jerry explained.

"Your teacher turned your hair blue?"

"Just ask the rest of the kids. Ms. Merriweather's

really weird. And she's mean. She even has a door named Sidney and—"

"She turned your hair blue?" Jerry's father interrupted.

"Yes, Dad."

"Why would she do that to me?"

"Maybe she doesn't want you to be reelected," suggested Jerry.

"That must be it."

"What are you going to do about it, Dad?"

"What's her name? Warrymeather?"

"Merriweather, Dad."

"Whatever. I'll get to the bottom of this. You can bet your blue roots on that," Jerry's dad promised.

"Good, Dad. Get her. Get her good."

"You can count your cookies I will. Ms. Cherryfeather won't know what hit her. She'll regret the day she ever challenged Finius Q. Sands." Jerry's father was getting excited. So was Jerry.

"Get her, Daddy!" urged Jerry. "Get her really, really, really good!"

"I'll rattle her rulers. I'll mangle her mind."

"I love you, Daddy."

"I'll teach that Ms. Carryleather a thing or two."

"Merriweather, Dad," Jerry corrected.

"Whatever. She'll wish she never heard of Darble-male School. Nothing stops Finius Q. Sands."

"All right, Dad!" Jerry cheered.

"I'll get to work on this right now. But first, would you please at least get that ribbon out of your hair?"

"I tried, Dad. It won't budge."

"That's ridiculous. Here, let me try." Jerry's father walked up to his son and yanked on the ribbon.

"Ouch!" Jerry cried. The ribbon stayed in place. Finius Q. Sands was left standing in his living room with a screaming son and a handful of blue hair.

Later that evening Lissie, Mitch, Kelly, and the Blue-haired Wonder got together. "This one is going to be tough," Lissie said.

"This one's different, all right," Mitch agreed.

"I kinda like this one," Kelly said softly, stroking her hair.

"This one's gone," Jerry vowed. Everyone looked at him. From the way Jerry's lips curled up on the sides of his mouth, everyone knew what had happened.

"You brought out the secret weapon?" Mitch asked.

"Yup," Jerry answered. "It's Daddy-time."

"Maybe you shouldn't have done that," Kelly said as she looked into a compact mirror to check her lipstick. "I think Ms. Merriweather is kinda neat."

"Kinda neat?" Jerry shouted, glaring at Kelly. "Look at what she did to me!"

Jerry tried to straighten out his blue pin curls, but whenever he let go of his hair, the curls would pop back into place.

Kelly kept looking in the mirror. "I don't know, Jer. I think blue just might be your color."

This is not the right thing to say to a person with blue pin curls. Jerry reached out and knocked the compact from Kelly's hands. "Look, little Ms. Perfect, how would you like it if tomorrow she turned your hair blue? Or maybe even made it fall out? Or grow out of your nose? Or—"

Things were getting out of hand. Mitch stepped between Jerry and Kelly. "Chill out, Jer. Aren't we all in this together?"

"I don't know. Ask the teacher-loving traitor, little Ms. Makeup."

"Shut up, Jerry. That's not fair," Mitch said. "Kelly's one of us. Now we just sit tight and let your

37

dad handle it. Okay?" Mitch looked around at his friends. "Okay?"

"Okay," echoed each in turn.

"Okay," Mitch repeated. "Let's shake on it." At that point all four started shaking their arms, legs, heads, and bodies until they fell to the ground. It was the official Room 104 shake.

Mitch and Kelly lived on the same street, so after the meeting they walked home together. As they reached Kelly's house, Mitch said, "Boy, Jerry sure was mad."

"I guess blue hair will do that to you," Kelly replied. "I just wish he hadn't gotten so mad at me. I was only kidding about blue being his color. Actually he's more of a yellow person."

"Don't worry about Jerry, Kel. He'll cool down. His father knows how to take care of business."

"I feel a little sad about that," Kelly told him. "I think Ms. Merriweather might be okay."

"You know what, Kelly?" Mitch said softly. "Don't tell Jerry, but I do too."

* * *

While all this was happening, Jerry's father was making a call. One ring . . . two rings . . . "Come on. Come on," he muttered impatiently. "Answer the phone!"

After the fourth ring a strange, almost ear-splitting, high-pitched voice came on the line. "Helloooo!" The voice crooned. "I'm dreadfully sorry that we are unable to respond to your summons at the moment. Do leave a kindly message after the annoying beep. Thank you ever so much."

"Dupas!" Finius screamed into the receiver after the beep. "Get on the phone—now!"

Before Finius finished his scream, a nervous male voice came on the line. "Um, ahhh, hi, Mr. Sands. This is Tiny."

"Get Scarlet on the phone. I need to talk with both of you."

Scarlet Dupa picked up an extension. It had been her voice on the answering machine. "Helloooo, Finius darling. How are you, my dear?"

"Shut up and listen." Finius told the Dupas the whole sordid, blue-haired story.

Scarlet and Tiny Dupa were teachers at Marbledale School. They were quite a sight to behold. Tiny's real name was Harry. But because he was six feet four inches tall and weighed 333 pounds, one of his students nicknamed him Tiny—and the name stuck. Scarlet, on the other hand, stood only four feet six inches, in heels, and tipped the scale at 88 pounds, dripping wet. Tiny had a reputation for being nasty. Scarlet was just plain mean.

Finius got them their jobs because no other school district in the country wanted to hire the Dupas. They had lost their previous teaching positions when it was discovered that Tiny could hardly spell his own name and Scarlet had trouble multiplying two times seven. But Finius saw the Dupas as an opportunity. An opportunity to hire a couple of people who would have to do anything he told them to.

"A school board member has to know what's going on in the schools. And what better way than to spy," he'd said on more than one occasion. The Dupas would do his bidding. They owed him a favor. They owed him their jobs.

"So," Finius said into the phone, "I want you two to find out what's going on in Room 104. I want all the dirt. If you can't find any, make some up. I want a reason to boot that teacher's bottom right out of the district."

The Dupas were perfect for the job.

40

*   *   *

That night Jerry dreamed of revenge. Mitch dreamed he was the commander of the *Enterprise*. Lissie dreamed about flying. And Kelly dreamed she had won a contest and had five minutes to scoop up anything she wanted from the makeup store at the mall, for free.

Meanwhile Ms. Franklin once again dreamed of being in the sixth grade. Again she woke up just as she raised her hand to ask a question.

CHAPTER FIVE

More of Ms. Merriweather's Mysteries

"**W**hat is that?" Jerry snarled as he and his friends filed into Room 104 the next morning. Everyone looked in the direction Jerry was pointing. The back wall of the classroom had been transformed into a giant mural of animals in an extremely colorful jungle. A large white deer with huge antlers stared out from the center of the work. Above him, two giant rabbits danced. A swan sat silently on the righthand side. Below her, three fawns slept. A little blue man sat cross-legged in the lefthand corner. He had a pile of gold coins in his hands and a banana in his mouth.

The rest of the mural was made up of a squirrel, a peacock, a red frog on a purple lily pad, various tropical birds, a wild boar, three turtles, and an array of flowers in reds, yellows, greens, purples, and pinks. The flowers were so bright that they seemed almost real. Indeed, this morning Room 104 did have a sweeter scent than usual.

When Ms. Merriweather walked in, she giggled. She immediately walked up to the mural and ran her hand over the deer's head as if she were petting it. "Well, Sidney was certainly busy last night."

"What's with the little blue dude?" Mitch asked. "He matches Jerry's hair." Jerry pulled the Detroit Tigers baseball cap he was wearing down over his ears to hide his blue perm and pink ribbon.

Ms. Merriweather walked over to the little blue man. "Oh, he was the last of the Gimmemorenows, a fierce tribe made up of people who would stop at nothing to get what they wanted—when they wanted it. Many years ago the tribe broke up and moved to cities around the world. Most of them became lawyers, politicians, or advertising executives."

Ms. Merriweather moved to the side so that everyone could see the entire mural. "Actually," she continued, "Sidney has given you quite a gift. All of the animals pictured here are quite extinct. Many, many years ago the snow deer of Tiaiaria, the giant rabbits of Nim, the mud turtles and golden peacocks of Paropador were all hunted for food, feathers, fur, or what some considered fun."

"I've never heard of any of those places," Lissie said. "Where are Tiaiaria, Nim, and Paropa-whatever?"

"New Jersey," Kelly called out. The class laughed.

"Oh, you won't find any of those places on maps anymore," Ms. Merriweather explained. "Like these extinct animals, they simply no longer exist. Their people lived . . . but they didn't learn.

"I've got a dog, and he really estinks," Mitch offered with a laugh. "What is *extinct*, anyway?"

"Extinct, my dear Mitchell," Ms. Merriweather replied as she walked back to her desk, "is what you'll be if you continue interrupting me."

Lissie noticed that the red liquid in the thermometer had risen from *cool* to *warm*. But Mitch was on a roll. "My sister ran across a skunk once, and she estinked for a week." He laughed. Now everyone

44

watched the thermometer rise from *warm* to *annoyed*.

"But then again, my sister always estinks. One time she estank so badly, they gave out gas masks in her birthday party goody bags." Mitch was getting a major league kick out of himself.

Ms. Merriweather sat silently with her hands folded on her desk. The thermometer rose to *angry*. Then the liquid started to bubble as it approached *I can't be responsible for what I might do now*. A hot breeze started to blow through the room. Mitch told how his sister estank so much that she was condemned and boarded up by the health department.

"Stop!" Ms. Merriweather rose from her desk. Mitch was startled by the strength in her voice. "I think you all should know," she said, clipping each word, "that this is no ordinary thermometer you see behind me. In fact, it's not a thermometer at all. It's a teacherometer. It measures my temper. And as you can see, my temper is almost at the boiling point."

She walked up to Mitch and put her hand on his left shoulder. "Now, you can continue with your little estink, estank, estunk act, and test the teacherometer. Or you can stop now and not regret later. I leave the decision entirely in your hands." Ms.

Merriweather kept her hand on his shoulder. The kids saw smoke coming from the teacherometer. Mitch looked at the blue curls popping out from under Jerry's baseball cap. He looked into Ms. Merriweather's eyes. He made a wise and prudent decision.

"The end," he said quickly, and looked down at his desk.

Meanwhile the Dupas were on the job. Scarlet and Tiny were wandering through the halls. They both were supposed to be teaching their own students, but once again couldn't find their classrooms. Tiny was munching on a piece of pizza he had found in the backseat of their car. Scarlet bit down hard on a toothpick.

Since they couldn't find their classrooms, the Dupas decided to check out Room 104. They knew it was straight ahead and to the right . . . or was it left? The Dupas were never very good with directions.

"What did Finius say that teacher's name was?" Tiny asked, spitting out little pieces of pepperoni as he spoke. "Was it Barryheather? Derrypeather?"

"I think it was Ferryveather," Scarlet answered.

"Why is Finius so mad at her?" Tiny wondered aloud.

"Didn't you hear what he told us on the phone?"

"Nah. I never listen to Finius," Tiny replied. "I just do what he says."

Scarlet was puzzled. "How can you do what he says to do without listening to him say it?"

"I guess I listen a little, but only when he starts to yell."

"Then you hear most of what he says, anyway," Scarlet said.

"Yeah," her husband agreed. "He yells a lot. Gives me a headache."

"Well, something else will ache if we don't get some real dirt on that teacher, like Finius says."

"Not to worry," Tiny said as they made yet another wrong turn. "I'll get the dirt on her real fast."

Scarlet looked impressed. "Really? How?"

"With this." Tiny pulled a small shovel and a plastic bag filled with mud out of his pants pocket.

"Not that kind of dirt, Dupa!"

"There's another kind?" Tiny was genuinely confused.

"Let me explain."

"Okay, but no big words. I'm only an English teacher, you know."

After making a couple of wrong turns and walking all the way around the school—twice—the Dupas finally reached Room 104.

"Let's take a peek. Me first," Tiny said.

"Me first," Scarlet said while trying to push Tiny out of the way.

"No, me!"

"No, me!"

"I'll flip you for it," Tiny offered.

"Okay," Scarlet agreed.

Tiny then flipped Scarlet across the hall and into the custodian's closet. When she stumbled out, her head was stuck in the bucket the custodian used to wash the floors.

"Heads ... I win." Tiny declared. He turned around and peeked into the room. "Wow! What a mess!" he exclaimed. When he looked into Room 104, he saw some kids playing catch with erasers and others rolling along the floor making dog noises.

"Let me see!" Scarlet yanked the bucket off her head with a loud pop, and crawled up Tiny's back. She saw an entirely different group of students—but with similar behavior. Scarlet laughed as she watched a girl with red hair going through the teacher's desk and two boys wrestling in the corner. "Look at those kids having a sword fight with red licorice sticks."

Tiny was looking and laughing, too. "How about that kid bouncing a tennis ball off the ceiling?"

"I don't see any tennis match," Scarlet replied with a snicker. "But check out the girl putting polka dots on that boy's face with the teacher's markers."

"Where? I don't see her," Tiny said. "But look at the boy using the teacher's work sheets for paper airplanes."

"There's no one doing that. I do see a boy carving his initials on the teacher's chair." Scarlet was all smiles. "This woman has no control at all." Scarlet pounded on Tiny's head. "She calls herself a teacher? Why, she's not even in her classroom."

"Yeah." Tiny pressed his nose up against the glass. "Just look at that kid catapulting paper clips with his ruler. Hold on. Wait a minute." Tiny got a more confused look than usual on his face. "That kid looks familiar."

"Eh, they all look alike to me," Scarlet said. "Look at the one at the blackboard, drawing a picture of the teacher. Look at the witch's hat. Hey, this should be good—she's writing something under the picture. Can you make it out, Tiny?"

"There's nobody at the blackboard," Tiny replied.

"Of course there is." Scarlet whapped Tiny on the top of his head with her hand. "Wait. She's making the words bigger. They say: "Ms. Dupa is a dufus.' " Scarlet's mouth dropped wide open.

All of a sudden Tiny's mouth hung wide open, too. "That kid with the ruler ... he looks like Tommy Harrison from my class."

"Tommy, schmommy," Scarlet grumbled. "That girl at the blackboard is Milly O'Lay from my class."

When the Dupas had looked into the window on the door to Room 104, Tiny had seen what was actually happening in his own classroom at that exact time, and Scarlet had seen what was happening in hers. They couldn't believe their eyes ... but they could believe their ears.

"Don't you two have somewhere you should be, like maybe your classrooms?" The voice behind the Dupas sounded firm and annoyed. The Dupas tumbled backward. Scarlet fell from Tiny's back. Tiny tripped over her and landed with a loud crash on his rather substantial bottom.

"M . . . M . . . M . . . Ms. Franklin," Tiny stuttered.

Scarlet rose quickly. "Good morning, Ms. Franklin. We were just going to welcome the new teacher to our delightful learning establishment—which, I must say, you run very well indeed."

"I'm sure you were," Ms. Franklin said sarcastically. "I believe you 'teachers' have your own students to attend to."

"That's just what I was telling Tiny," Scarlet replied. "Isn't that right, dear?"

Tiny scratched his head. "I don't remember your saying . . . " Scarlet gave him a quick, but painful, kick in the shin. It seemed to jar his memory. "Oh, yeah," Tiny said, rubbing his leg. "Now I remember." The Dupas started backing down the hall, away from Ms. Franklin.

"Good to see you, Ms. Franklin," Scarlet said.

"Let's do lunch," Tiny offered.

Ms. Franklin sighed. "Why me?" She was about to go back to her office, when she decided to take a peek into Room 104 herself. "I'm the principal. I have a right to know what's going on." She was also getting a little concerned. It was awfully quiet in Room 104.

Ms. Franklin put her face up to the window. "Oh,

51

my goodness!" she exclaimed as she peered through the glass. Ms. Franklin saw the new white desks and the mural. She saw the crystal globe and the teacherometer. It was what she didn't see that scared her. There were no students in Room 104. Ms. Franklin's eyes were drawn to an old white door frame with the name Sidney across the top. Sidney stood wide open.

CHAPTER SIX

Just Another Day in Room 104

After a quick look down the hall to make sure no one was watching, Ms. Franklin opened the door to Room 104 and slowly walked into the studentless classroom. Part of her felt as though she were twelve years old again and didn't want to get caught sneaking into class late. Once inside she slowly looked around. This was no ordinary classroom. Everything sparkled, from the starship *Enterprise* to the glistening blackboard. The blackboard looked as if it had just been washed, but when Ms. Franklin touched it, it was completely dry.

She walked up to Sidney and was about to close him when she distinctly heard: "Na-uh-uh, Barbara. You know better than that." Ms. Franklin jerked around, expecting to see somebody standing right behind her. But all she saw were the desks and the mural.

Everything was so odd, and yet oddly familiar. Somewhere, a long time ago, Ms. Franklin was sure she had seen a similar room. It was like a dream. Could it be a dream? Ms. Franklin thought. I might be dreaming. I have to be dreaming. Okay, I am dreaming. Now, seeing as I'm dreaming, I should be able to do anything I want.

Ms. Franklin reasoned: If you know you're dreaming, you really can do just about anything you can imagine. Once you know you're dreaming, you're in control of that dream. You can lift the Empire State Building, swim the Atlantic Ocean, fly. Ms. Franklin decided to try dream number 3. She climbed up on Lissie's desk. "This is a dream," she muttered again and again. "This is a dream." She jumped off, hoping to fly around the room.

This was no dream.

The principal of Marbledale School came crashing back to wide-awake earth. It was a short flight—

straight down. It was not a soft landing. When Ms. Franklin hit the floor, she slightly twisted her right ankle. She didn't know whether to scream in pain or cringe in embarrassment over her attempt to take off. Ms. Franklin sat down at the desk and rubbed her ankle. She looked at the swelling. "Yup. This is real, all right."

Ms. Franklin forgot about her ankle and concentrated on the current crisis she was facing. Where were Mitch, Lissie, Jerry, Kelly, and all the rest of the students who were supposed to be sitting at these desks? "Ms. Merriweather, what did you do?" she asked aloud. Ms. Franklin put her head in her hands. She felt her stomach tightening into a knot the size of a two-ton boulder. "What in the world is going on?"

When Ms. Franklin looked up from her hands, her eyes were drawn to the blackboard and the message that now appeared on it.

"Piddle-dee diddle-dee. You worry so much. You just go and take care of your principaling and leave Room 104 to me." The message was signed: "M. M."

The principal blinked her eyes and shook her head. Now she read, "P.S. Better put some ice on that ankle."

Ms. Franklin got up and started to leave. She turned back to the blackboard to read the message one more time. "It must have been there when I walked in, and I just didn't notice it." But when Ms. Franklin took her second look, the blackboard was once again sparkling clean, as if it had just been washed.

Earlier, before Ms. Franklin's attempt to fly, it had been a busy morning in Room 104. It didn't take Ms. Merriweather long to discover that, for this particular group of students, thinking was the last thing on their minds. Math just didn't add up. English seemed like a foreign language. And when it came to reading, the book was closed.

Mitch started flicking spitballs at another kid, but stopped when each spitball reversed course in midair and ended up stuck to his own forehead. "Seems as though life has thrown you a curve," Ms. Merriweather commented as Mitch tried to pry the little wads of paper from his head.

Lissie secretly (or so she thought) unwrapped a piece of grape bubble gum and popped it into her mouth. When Ms. Merriweather wasn't looking, she'd blow a quick bubble and snap it back with a loud click. Her fun didn't last very long.

Once, after the blow and before the snap, Ms. Merriweather turned around and made eye-to-bubble contact. Lissie tried snapping it back fast, but the bubble wouldn't budge. In fact, the harder she sucked in, the bigger the bubble grew. Ms. Merriweather kept staring as the bubble grew to the size of a baseball . . . then a basketball . . . then a beach ball.

Lissie stood up next to her desk, her eyes as wide as saucers. She tried to pull the gum from her mouth, but the bubble was now so big that she couldn't even reach her lips. The bubble just kept growing. Soon it was the size of a purple weather balloon.

There was no telling how big it might have gotten if Ms. Merriweather hadn't clapped her hands and said, "I hate to burst your bubble, dear, but . . . "

There was a loud explosion. Everyone except Lissie dived for the floor, hands covering ears. When the kids looked up after the blast, Lissie was coated from head to toe with what looked like sticky, purple slime.

"But"—Ms. Merriweather continued where she'd

left off—"the next time you want to chew gum in class, make sure you have enough for everyone." Ms. Merriweather turned to the rest of the class. "I love saying that. It sounds so . . . so teachery, don't you think?"

Lissie wasn't listening. She was trying to pull gum from her face. But she couldn't. The gum stuck to her fingers. As she pulled her hands away from her face, long, gooey strings of stuff stretched from her fingers to her nose, mouth, cheeks, and chin. "Help."

"That's what I'm here for," Ms. Merriweather said as she pulled a small golden hanky from her vest and walked toward the new Ms. Gumby.

"That little thing won't help," Mitch grumbled. He was trying to pry the spitballs from his forehead with the end of a ruler.

"Don't judge what you don't know, Mitchell," Ms. Merriweather said. When she walked by Mitch, she gently brushed the hanky across his forehead. The spitballs were gone. Ms. Merriweather walked up to Lissie and felt the gooey guck that filled her hair. "Quite the sticky wicket you've gotten yourself into, my dear."

"Please help," Lissie begged.

"No more bubble trouble?" Ms. Merriweather asked.

Lissie shook her head no.

"Very well then." Ms. Merriweather ran the hanky over Lissie. In a flash the gum was gone. Ms. Merriweather shook out the hanky, which was also completely clean.

On the third shake something fell from the hanky to the floor. "Ah." Ms. Merriweather sighed. "I knew it had to be in there somewhere." With that, she picked up a piece of grape bubble gum. It was fully wrapped. "You can reclaim your chew toy later, Lissie . . . after school."

It was a typical morning in Room 104. As usual the students had no intention of using their minds on such meaningless matters as mathematics. Kelly spent more time looking into her pocket mirror than at the lesson on the blackboard. Jerry spent his time glaring angrily at Ms. Merriweather as he kept trying to shove all his blue hair under his hat.

Finally Ms. Merriweather had had enough. She put her fingers to her lips and let out the loudest whistle ever heard. Everyone jumped. Even the desks shook, and the starship *Enterprise* started swinging from its invisible string. Ms. Merriweather seemed to be a bit embarrassed.

"Sorry. I hated to do that. But it does seem to be quite the attention getter." Everyone's attention now secured, Ms. Merriweather continued ... softly. "All of your other teachers were correct. You, my dears, are completely, totally, and undeniably ... unteachable."

Ms. Merriweather wasn't angry. Her voice sounded like silk, but her words were as hard as steel. "You are contrary and cantankerous, difficult and devilish, ornery and obstinate." No one knew what to think about this latest development. Never had a teacher talked to them in this manner.

"Not to mention roguish and rowdy." Ms. Merriweather looked from student to student. "There is not a teacher on earth ... or elsewhere ... who could teach you anything in your present states of mindlessness."

No one else said a single word. Ms. Merriweather had plenty of them to go around. "The problem with you, my dear 104iors, is that you simply do not think. And the consequences of not thinking are severe indeed. You must think before you act. Every action we take in life causes its own unique reaction.

Positive action generally leads to positive reaction, and vice versa."

Ms. Merriweather walked over to the door named Sidney. "Many people go through their entire lives without thinking. They begin as thoughtless little children and end up as thoughtless little adults. It could happen to you."

She slowly opened Sidney. "So before anyone can teach you, before you can learn, you must learn to think. And you must fully comprehend what could happen if you don't."

Ms. Merriweather looked at all the confused faces before her. "You still don't understand, I know. But you will . . . soon. Follow me," she called out in a loud voice as she stepped through Sidney . . . and vanished.

Meanwhile, despite the confrontation with Ms. Franklin, the Dupas had decided against going back to their classrooms. (Not that they could have found them, anyway.) Instead they raced out of the school building to a nearby store that had a pay phone. While Tiny bought some Twinkies, Scarlet placed a call to Finius Q. Sands.

One ring ... two rings ... "Where is that fink-faced Fini—"

"Hello. This is Finius Q. Sands," boomed his voice from an answering machine. The "Star-Spangled Banner" started to play in the background as the message continued. "Finius Q. Sands ... a man of the people. A man who's running for a well-de-served second term on the school board. A man who's always there for you, whenever you need him. I'm sorry I can't come to the phone right now. Leave your message after the beep, and remember ... a vote for Finius Q. Sands is a vote for ... me."

"Hello, Finius. Scarlet Dupa here. I wanted to tell you that—"

"This better be good, Dupa." The live version of Finius had picked up the phone. He sounded angry, and half asleep. "I was just taking a nap. I was dreaming that I was president, and had just ordered that my face replace that George What's-his-name's on the one-dollar bill." Scarlet nervously tapped her foot as Finius continued. "And the photographer had just arrived to take my picture for the Finius Q. Sands postage stamp."

Scarlet waited silently for him to finish. She knew that it was a very bad idea to interrupt Finius when he answered the phone during one of his several naps. She knew it could be a long wait. Two weeks earlier Finius had gone on for an hour and a half about a dream in which he was the emperor of Rome, and how he had put a roof on the Coliseum and called it the Q-Dome. A month before that he had had a Marie Antoinette dream. Scarlet had dared to interrupt him while he was in the middle of her famous "Let them eat cake" line. He had ordered her to the guillotine.

But this time she had real news. At considerable risk to life and limb, Scarlet interrupted Finius just as he was telling how he had dumped the eagle as the nation's symbol and replaced it with his parakeet, Genghis. "Finius, Finius, I'm sorry to—"

"How dare you interrupt your president!" Finius had dozed off again. He was talking in his sleep. "I have Congress to deal with, the Supreme Court, the people who elected me and actually expect me to keep my promises."

"Finius!" Scarlet said loudly—not to mention bravely. "Finius, wake up!"

"And then there's the White House gatekeeper who won't let me in."

"Wake up, Finius!" Scarlet screamed.

"What? Who? Where? Is it time for school? I'm sick, Mommy. My tummy aches. Ohhhhhhhhh-hhh."

"Finius, this is Scarlet Dupa. Wake all the way up."

Finius woke up. "This better be good, Dupa. I was just taking a nap. I was dreaming I was president of the United States and . . . "

"I know, Finius. I know."

"Anyway, did you get the dirt on that Ms. Garyzeather?"

"Well, not exactly, but—"

"Exactly what do you mean by not exactly? Didn't Tiny bring the shovel and mud I gave him?"

"Finius, there's something crazy going on there. I think that classroom might be, at the very least, haunted." Scarlet told Finius what had happened. As she told him, Tiny stood by the cash register and tried to see how many Twinkies he could get in his mouth at one time.

When Scarlet had finished the story, and after the store owner performed the Heimlich maneuver on Tiny, Finius was angrier then ever. "How dare you waste my time on the telephone," he screamed. "I don't care if you saw your life's story in that window. Get back to that classroom. Find out what's going on. Get that teacher. Get her good!"

"You got it, boss." Scarlet didn't sound very convincing. She was still a little shaken over what they had seen through the window to Room 104.

"I want results!" Finius was still screaming. "I am a very busy man! Now leave me alone. It's time for my next naaa . . . meeting." Finius hung up the phone. Scarlet looked at Tiny, who had switched from Twinkies to chocolate cupcakes and root beer.

"Let's go get the job done the way only a Dupa can," she called to her husband as he chewed and slurped.

"Yeah. Let's get her!" Tiny yelled, his mouth wide open.

The store owner covered his own mouth, bent over, and ran from the room. Even Scarlet felt a little queasy. Both had a perfect view through Tiny's crumb-covered lips into a messy mouthful of chewed up cupcake and root beer. It was not a pretty sight.

CHAPTER SEVEN

The World Beyond Sidney

As soon as Ms. Merriweather had disappeared through Sidney, Jerry cheered. "All right! We finally got rid of her!" Nobody else moved. Jerry started dancing on his desk. "Lock that door and throw away the key!"

"What does she mean, we don't know how to think?" Lissie wondered out loud.

"*I* think she's a nut," the boy named Ian said.

"Takes one to know one," Kelly teased.

"Peanut-brain," Ian muttered in response.

Kelly turned up her nose in disgust. "Well, I think

we should do exactly what Ms. Merriweather said and—"

"You are crazy, Kelly." Jerry jumped off his desk. "It's our big chance to get rid of her once and for all. Did you forget the pledge we took?" Jerry looked around at his classmates. "Have you all forgotten?" Jerry pulled Mitch up from his desk. "Come on, Mitch. Do it with me."

"Mitch rather reluctantly put out his hands. As they began chanting the pledge, they started slapping each other's hands, alternating right to left and left to right.

> They call us nasty and they call us mean.
> We're the worst that they've ever seen.
> Hey, Yo, teacher, we think you're a bore.
> You're out the door to Room 104.

They continued to slap and clap in rhythm.

We don't do homework. We won't take no tests.
You might want a pet . . . but we're teacher's pests.
Bring out a book and we declare war.
You're out the door to Room 104.

They both yelled and thrust their fists into the air.

104 . . . LET'S ROAR!

Mitch and Jerry ended the pledge with a double high five as the class cheered. Kelly stood her ground. "Maybe we should change the pledge."

Everyone turned and stared at Kelly. No one looked particularly friendly. She shifted her weight nervously from one foot to the other and back again. "Well, um, what I mean, um . . . um . . . um . . . "

"The teacher lover can't even talk." Jerry laughed. "Um . . . um . . . um . . . Jerry tried to sound like a gorilla while mocking Kelly.

"What I mean," Kelly said clearly, "is that maybe we should give her a chance. It might be fun."

Jerry was now jumping around the room, still making his gorilla sounds. Kelly was angry, very angry. She knew her face was turning bright red, which only made her angrier. She did not like how she looked in red. "Jerry, you're such a jerk," she yelled as she stomped her feet. "A jelly-brained, chicken-face jerk!"

"Who you calling a chick—" Jerry didn't get a

68

"I can't have any fun around here anymore."

Jerry could have sworn he then heard a loud, disappointed groan as he stopped in midair, half an inch from the wall.

"Bring him back now, Sidney." It was Ms. Merriweather's voice again. "Be a good boy."

"Be a good boy, Sidney. Be a good boy, Sidney. That's all I ever hear. Be a good boy, Sidney. Fine. You want him—you got him."

Jerry wasn't sure if Ms. Merriweather said anything in reply . . . he was too busy screaming. He was moving again, faster and faster. But this time he was being pulled directly toward Sidney. "No!" he screamed, watching the door open wider and wider as he was sucked closer and closer. A moment later Jerry flew through the door and was gone.

It was only seconds after Jerry vanished that Ms. Franklin had entered Room 104, conducted her experiment in dream flight, and received the message on the blackboard. Afterward she had started walking slowly down the hall toward her office. She never made it. About halfway there she had turned and walked out the school door to her car.

Her ankle was slightly swollen, and there was a

twinge of pain as she slid into the driver's seat. "I'd better get my ice pack," she said out loud as she turned on the ignition and started her car.

She tried to convince herself that she was only going home to pick up the ice pack and an ace bandage for her ankle. Deep inside she knew better. In her mind she kept seeing Room 104—the white desks, the crystal globe. She couldn't shake the feeling that she had been in that room before . . . many years ago.

So while Ms. Franklin tried to think of where she might have put her ice pack, she was aware that she was going home to find something else, something that would finally answer the question she'd been trying to ask each night in her dreams.

Meanwhile, back in the land of the lost Dupas, Scarlet was trying to teach Tiny a few manners. "Don't talk with your mouth full, you slobbery sloth," Scarlet scolded as she and Tiny ran from the store, heading back to school. "It just ain't cultured."

Tiny spit the chewed-up cupcake and root beer from his mouth. It landed on the sidewalk with a loud *splut*. "That better?" he asked.

"Much. Thank you."

"You're welcome," Tiny said as he stuffed another whole cupcake into his mouth and slugged down the rest of his root beer. As they ran, Tiny belched out a question. "How are we going to get that Ms. Zerribeather?"

"We'll figure that out when we get there," Scarlet replied as she made a left turn and ran smack into a fire hydrant.

It took the Dupas almost an hour to get back to Marbledale School, even though it was less than two blocks from the store. They made a left turn when they should have made a right, and then a right when they should have made a left. If it weren't for the assistance of a helpful second-grader, they might still be wandering around town, arguing over which one had gotten them lost.

Once inside the school, they traveled around the halls for another twenty minutes before they were able to find Room 104. For them it was a new speed record. As they stood before the door, Scarlet, remembering what had happened earlier, said, "Tiny, you may have the honor of looking through the window first."

"No ... you." Tiny tried to sound superpolite.

"No, dear. You." Scarlet tried to outpolite him.

"I couldn't."

"I insist."

"No. You look first."

"You."

"You."

"You."

By the time they said "you" for the thirty-fourth and thirty-fifth times, the Dupas no longer sounded polite. They were screaming at each other. Finally both said "Fine!" Then they bonked their heads together as they tried to look into Room 104 at the same time. "Dupa!" they both yelled as they grabbed their heads.

"Forget the window," Scarlet ordered. "Let's just barge in and surprise that little toad of a teacher."

"I love surprises." Tiny snickered.

"I hope she doesn't," Scarlet said as she turned the knob and threw open the door.

"Surprise!" Tiny and Scarlet yelled as the door swung open and slammed into the wall. But the only ones to be surprised were the Dupas.

"Where'd they go?" Tiny asked, scratching his head and looking around the room.

"Maybe they went to the ice cream shop for triple-scoop fudge sundaes," Scarlet retorted.

"Without inviting me?" Tiny whined.

"How the hula hoop should I know where they went!" Scarlet gave Tiny a backhanded slap upside the head. (Actually the safest place to hit Tiny was on the head. You were sure of not damaging something important.) "Look around," Scarlet barked. "Find something. Find anything."

Scarlet went right to Ms. Merriweather's desk. She threw open the drawers. The only thing she found was a piece of grape bubble gum. Other than that, the drawers were completely empty.

"Just a stupid piece of gum," she called to Tiny, who was looking through the students' desks.

"Can I have it?" Tiny was in the mood for a good chew. In fact, Tiny was always in the mood for putting anything even close to edible into his mouth. With a disgusted look Scarlet tossed him the gum. He caught it one-handed. But when he opened his fingers, his hand was empty.

"Hey, what'd you do?" Tiny asked. Scarlet looked down. The gum was back in the drawer. There was a little note attached to it. It read: "Lissie's gum . . . Not for Dupas."

"I want gum! I want gum!" Tiny moaned.

"Forget the gum, bubble-brain." Scarlet slammed the drawer shut. "Keep looking around."

"I'll find my own gum," Tiny muttered as he started running his hands under the desks. "There's got to be some stuck under one of these."

"Well, if it isn't the big, bad Dupas." All at once a voice boomed through the room. Scarlet and Tiny jumped about two feet into the air.

"Who said that?" Scarlet demanded. Silence. The Dupas looked at each other and shrugged their shoulders.

"How are things in Dupaville?" The voice returned.

Tiny and Scarlet looked directly at the open door named Sidney. The voice was coming from the other side. The sound was as clear as a bell, but there was nothing on the other side of the door. At least nothing they could see.

Suddenly they heard circus music and a voice like the ones you hear at a carnival sideshow. "Ladies and gentlemen and Dupas of all ages. Step right up. Step right up and see things to marvel and amaze. Hurry! Hurry! Hurry!"

"What the bumper pool is going on?" Scarlet had

to scream out her question in order to be heard over the music and the raspy voice.

"Come in and see. It's beyond belief." The voice continued. "And it's all yours for only a nickel. Count 'em—five little cents. Step right up to the door, Dupas. Step through and become part of the greatest show on earth."

Scarlet and Tiny walked up to Sidney and looked in, while the carnival music played on. "What kind of sneaky trick is this?" Tiny asked.

"She must have a tape recorder somewhere in there," Scarlet reasoned. "Find it . . . and wreck it."

"Yeah." Tiny smiled. "Let's wreck it."

They both tried to go through Sidney, but bounced back. It was as if they'd walked into a rubber wall. "Your nickels, please," the voice called out.

Tiny and Scarlet grumbled, but dug through their pockets. They tossed two nickels into Sidney. The coins vanished in a flash of light. "Thank you," the voice said. "And I hope your stay will be a pleasant one."

The next moment the Dupas were yanked through Sidney, and the classroom was again empty.

CHAPTER EIGHT

Into the Future

As soon as Kelly took that first angry step through Sidney, she entered a world without form or foundation. There was no up. There was no down. No left . . . no right. It was a world of everything and nothing, substance and smoke.

She thought she was slowly turning . . . but maybe not. There was no way to really tell. Around her, colors swirled—purples, reds, blues, greens, golds. The colors mixed and separated, spinning together before pulling apart. It was as if Kelly were in an ocean of paint of every imaginable hue, but all she felt was cool, refreshing air. It felt good. Kelly was no longer angry with Jerry and his ape noises. Kelly was smiling.

As she traveled through the silent sea of color, Kelly would occasionally see a face, a time. Her grandmother's face appeared and was gone. Her kindergarten teacher's. Some faces she'd never seen before. Sometimes only eyes would float by. Sometimes only smiles. Kelly thought she should be frightened, but she felt oddly secure.

For a moment Kelly was only two years old . . . then she was seventeen. Time moved in moments past and memories still to come. Kelly saw doors— many, many doors. They floated by in swirls of color. Turning and slowly flipping past her. Hundreds of doors. Maybe thousands.

Kelly had no way of knowing it at the time, but the same thing was happening to every student who had gone through Sidney. Colors and faces. Dreams and doors. Each saw himself or herself at different times. Past and future blended into the present.

Each also heard Ms. Merriweather's voice.

Refuse to think and you will see,
this is what perhaps could be.

Tumbling, jumbling, twisting like tops.
Life is a series of moments and stops.

Dreams and visions. Magic and maps.
Sparkles, shimmers, glimmers, and snaps.
If you're wise, you'll win.
If not, you'll lose.
Doors . . . doors . . . doors . . .
Which one will you choose?

Ms. Merriweather's voice sounded like a lullaby. Kelly closed her eyes. When she opened them, all the colors were gone. She stood facing a single, pure white door. Kelly reached out, gently pushed it open, and stepped inside. Kelly was surprised by what she saw.

There were no swirling colors or illusions. No magic smoke or gusts of wind. Kelly saw only herself . . . a reflection in a mirror. Kelly laughed and straightened out her hair. Well, if this is my future, she thought, I must say I'm going to look pretty good.

Kelly had a little routine she'd do whenever she was in front of a mirror . . . which was usually at least twice an hour. First she'd straighten her hair. Then she'd flip it back, giving a big smile, the way those models on magazine covers do. This was always followed by a series of poses, ranging from pouts to puckers. Finally Kelly would straighten her hair again, kiss her fingers, and place them on the mirror. "What can I say?" she asked her reflection. "We're perfect."

Kelly followed her routine to the letter. But as she turned to walk away, she bopped her nose into a pane of glass. "Ouch," Kelly cried. She turned and tried to walk in the other direction. This time her forehead struck glass. She tried to step backward, but again hit glass.

She looked ahead, and her reflection looked back. She saw herself kiss her fingers. She felt it when what she thought was her reflection touched her lips. Kelly watched in horror as her image waved and walked away. She put her hands up to the glass. "Let me out! Let me out!" she shouted. Kelly was no longer just looking at the mirror. She was in it . . . part of it . . . and couldn't escape. She heard Ms. Merriweather's voice.

> Your mind is a miracle.
> Imagination, a gift.
> The future is yours

to change or to shift.
Think hard, Kelly.
Think or you'll see
that you'll wind up a mere reflection
of what you could be.

When Mitch stopped spinning and opened his eyes, he stood facing a schoolroom door. He expected to see swirls of silver and rose, but all he saw was this old brown door. He looked up slowly. Above the door he saw the number 104.

"How did I get out here?" he said. "Some nice trick, Ms. M." Mitch reached out and opened the door. He might have noticed that his voice was a lot deeper and a little crackly had he not been stunned by the sound of sudden applause.

The room was full of sixth-graders. All of them were standing up and clapping for all they were worth. A male teacher walked toward Mitch. He, too, was applauding. "Mitch, Mitch." The teacher smiled and shook Mitch's hand. "This is the nineteen thousand seven hundred and tenth straight day you've been late for class. I'm glad you decided to end your career in the sixth grade the way it began."

End what career? Mitch thought as he looked

around the room. It was Room 104, all right. But without the white desks, posters, or Sidney. The students, none of whom Mitch recognized, were standing next to green, mushroom-shaped seats. Where the blackboard had been there was a clear glass panel. Strange mathematical equations appeared and disappeared in the blink of an eye. The symbols were like nothing Mitch had ever seen before.

The room was bright, but there were no lights anywhere. The brightness seemed to come from the ceiling itself. Finally Mitch's eyes saw something familiar . . . a calendar. The calendar had a picture of spaceships docking at a space station on it. Mitch looked down from the picture to the date. The day and month were right, but the year was fifty-four years from now.

Before Mitch could say a word, two of the students reached up and took him by each arm. "Come on, Mitch," one said. "Sit down. Take a load off those old bones."

"Old bones?" Mitch shouted. "What do you mean, old bones?" Mitch raised his fists. It was at that exact moment that he first noticed his hands. They were large and covered with freckles, gray hair, and wrinkles. A wedding band sparkled on the ring finger of his left hand. He stared at it as the two boys pushed him down into the largest mushroom seat in the class. It molded around his bottom in a perfect fit. A plastic desktop inflated in front of him, complete with books, papers, pencils, and pens.

But all Mitch was looking at was the ring. The teacher must have noticed, because he came up to Mitch and in a soft voice said, "I know how you must feel, Mitch. It would sure have been nice if your wife had lived long enough to see this day. She would have been so proud of you." The teacher patted him on the shoulder. "She should have realized that the guy who told her to 'go jump in the lake' didn't mean that she should actually do it." Mitch kept his eyes on the ring. My wife, Mitch thought. I have a wife?

"Oh, well. Life's life, eh, Mitch?" the teacher remarked in a happy voice. "On with the ceremony." The class cheered. The teacher called for silence. "Mitch, on this, your sixty-fifth birthday, we in Room 104 are proud to present you with a goldlike watch in recognition of your fifty-four years in sixth grade. We'll miss you, Mitch. We'll miss your snoring in class, your wrong answers, and, yes, even your occasional drooling problems."

"Oh, yuck!" A girl two mushrooms down moaned.

The teacher gave her a stern look. "If you were in the sixth grade for more than half a century, you might suffer from the agony of uncontrollable drooling yourself."

"Never!"

"Never say 'never,'" the teacher cautioned. "Mitch *never* studied, *never* worked, *never* did much of anything. And now"—the teacher clicked his tongue—"all old Mitch is left with is a cheap watch and a wet chin." The teacher turned back toward Mitch. "We wish you the best of luck as you finally, finally retire from Marbledale School."

"I'm only eleven years old!" Mitch tried to shout, but his voice was drowned out by all the students' screaming: "Speech! Speech!"

The teacher bent down close to Mitch's ear and whispered. "You do know what a speech is, don't you, Mitch?"

"Speech! Speech!" The screams grew louder and louder, then suddenly stopped. The kids stood frozen—their mouths wide open, stuck in mid-scream. The teacher stood like a statue, a fraction of an inch from Mitch's ear. Mitch could feel the teacher's scratchy whiskers, but he couldn't hear or feel him breathing.

What Mitch did hear was Ms. Merriweather's voice. He heard it quite clearly.

> Frozen in time,
> frozen in space,
> the future is yours
> to change or to face.
> Dry aging winds
> through icy days blow
> if you miss this . . . your chance
> to blossom and grow.

Lissie's eyes popped open in fright. As they had with Kelly and Mitch, the swirling colors had vanished. But Lissie was scared. Terrified. She stood facing a large, pitch-black marble door. She didn't want to go inside.

"Open the door, Lissie." She heard Ms. Merriweather's voice, but the teacher was nowhere in sight.

Lissie was shaking. "I'm not going in there."

"You must open the door, Lissie." The voice came from nowhere . . . or maybe everywhere.

"I don't have to." Lissie shuddered.

"You do."

"Do not."

"Do, too"

"Do not."

"Do, too."

"Not."

"Too."

"You open it yourself if you're so darn interested."

"I can't open it. Only you can." Ms. Merriweather urged her forward. "What could be your future lies beyond the door. Only you can open it."

Opening that black marble door was the last thing Lissie wanted to do. But she found herself reaching out and pushing. The door was very heavy. It barely moved. Lissie leaned against it with her shoulder and pushed. Slowly it swung open.

Lissie found herself in a large, gray room. A single light bulb hung from the ceiling above a table in the middle of the room. At the table two men were playing cards. There were long, narrow tables along the gray walls. Some of them were covered with white sheets. The sheets had something under them, but Lissie couldn't tell what.

She heard the two men talking. "Fish for all your kings," one said.

"Go fish," the other one said as he looked down at the two kings he was holding in his hands.

"You're cheating," the first one accused.

"I am not."

"I know you're cheating."

"How?"

"Because I peeked at your cards. I know you have two kings."

"Boy, you're good at this game," the man remarked while pulling out the two kings and giving them to his friend.

"Fish for all your tens." The first one said.

"Go fish." The second man looked down at the ten he was holding.

"You're cheating again."

"I am not."

Lissie tried to interrupt them. "Excuse me, but could you tell me where I am?"

The men kept arguing and playing their game, as if they hadn't heard a thing.

"Excuse me," Lissie repeated, this time in a louder voice. "Can you help me?"

The men didn't even blink. Lissie walked up to

them and tried to tap one on the shoulder to get his attention. Her hand passed right through him, as if it were nothing more than smoke.

"You win," the second man told the first as he handed over the last pair of threes. "You always win."

"Talent, my friend. Pure talent."

"Yeah, talent spelled C-H-E-A-T." Both men laughed. Lissie tried to touch one on his head. But again her hand went straight through and out the other side.

When the men stopped laughing, one of them asked the other, "What happened to that new one over there on table four?" He pointed with his thumb at the table in the far corner of the room. It was one of those with a white sheet.

"Oh, she came in last night."

"What's her story?"

"You're really not going to believe this, but somebody told her to go jump in a lake."

"And she did?"

The other man put his palms together and made a gesture as if he were diving into water. "Splush!"

"Couldn't she have tried to swim out?"

"Nope."

"Why not?"

"Didn't know how to swim."

"She jumped in a lake even though she didn't know how to swim?"

"Yup. Shame is, she once had a chance to start using her talents and her mind."

"Why didn't she take it?"

"Guess she didn't think it was important at the time."

"Didn't *think* is right."

Lissie tried to interrupt again. "Who are you guys talking about?" Again there was no answer.

"How about another game of cards?" The man who had won the previous games asked.

"Okay, but no more fish."

"Kid stuff," the first one said. "Let's play a real game. No holds barred. Cutthroat."

"You don't mean . . . "

"I do."

"But last time I got stuck with the old maid seven times in a row."

"Shut up and deal." The first man handed his friend a deck of cards. It was his own special deck, the one in which the old maid card had a secret crease in the corner.

Lissie was about to ask them another question, but realized it wouldn't do any good. Her eyes were drawn to the table in the corner, the one they had called table four. Everything else in the room became fuzzy and out of focus. Only the table, with its white sheet, was in clear sight. She slowly took one small step toward the table . . . then another . . . and another.

Soon she found herself standing at the foot of the table. A tag hung out from under the sheet. She reached out and lifted it up into the dim light. There were few words on the tag. All Lissie saw was her name, followed by the letters *DOA*.

Everything faded to black as Lissie listened to Ms. Merriweather's voice.

> Darkness so deep,
> all colors turn black.
> A quicksand of shadows,
> there's no going back.
> But your tomorrow's still future
> to model and mold.
> A living rainbow of colors
> can be yours to hold.

*　　*　　*

Jerry's eyes had stayed closed from the moment he was sucked into Sidney. His eyes were shut tight, but his mouth was wide open. "Help! NOOOO! Get me out of here!" Other phrases, not normally used in polite conversation, streamed from his mouth like lava from a volcano.

Jerry didn't see the swirling colors, the faces, the eyes, or the doors as he spun toward his possible future. Even when he stopped spinning, he kept screaming.

"Put a sock in it," Jerry heard a voice say, just before something was stuffed into his open mouth. Now Jerry's eyes were wide open. He reached to his mouth and pulled out a rather attractive blue and yellow argyle sock. It was tied to a white athletic sock with purple stripes along the top, which was followed by a black silk sock, a blue knee-length, two red anklets, a green dress sock, and finally a pair of opaque panty hose.

Jerry was furious. "I'll get you for this, Sidney . . . you dirty . . . stinking—"

"I said, zip it," the voice interrupted.

Sure enough, Jerry's last words became nothing more than a mumble. His mouth was zipped up tight. Jerry pulled his zipper-lips from left to right, only to find them still zipped, and then from right to left. He must have unzipped from right to left and then left to right a dozen times before he was finally able to pull his lips apart. It sounded like Velcro separating when he opened his mouth to speak.

"Don't say anything, Jerry." Now it was Ms. Merriweather's voice that he heard. "I think Sidney is getting tired of being so nice." Jerry took the advice. Instead of cursing, he just growled softly.

"Open the door, Jerry. Open the door," Ms. Merriweather's voice coaxed.

For the first time Jerry noticed that he was standing in front of a door. It was one he recognized in a second. It was the door to his father's office. Jerry smiled a mean little smile.

"I got you now," he said. "Wait until my dad hears about this." Jerry turned the knob and pushed open the door.

As he expected, Jerry found himself standing in his father's office. The familiar tattered couch with its cigar burns sat along one wall. The familiar moosehead hung over it, with its plaque bearing the slogan "Guns don't kill. I do."

Jerry approached his father's desk. The back of the

chair was turned toward him, but Jerry could see two shoeless feet resting on the windowsill. He could also hear loud snoring coming from the other side of the chair, a surefire sign that the feet on the sill belonged to his father.

"Dad, Dad. Wake up."

There was a snort from the front of the chair. "I'm the king . . . the king, I tell you," the sleepy voice mumbled.

Jerry walked up to the chair. "Wake up, Dad. Get a life, will you?"

Jerry spun the chair around. The man in it was not his father. This man was somewhat fatter and some-what balder, and had a scraggly beard. It looked as though he had dropped some lasagna on his bulging white shirt. He smelled really bad.

"What are you doing in my father's chair?" Jerry demanded.

The snoring mass of flesh and blubber just wheezed and gagged. "The queen of England," it muttered. "I am the queen of England." The man's head fell onto the desk with a loud thud. But he didn't wake up.

Jerry backed up a few steps. "Who are you?" he screamed.

The answer seemed to ooze from between the man's cracked lips. "I'm you" was all the man said before he belched and resumed his snoring. "I'm you."

Jerry turned and started to run. It was as if he were moving in slow motion, as if he were stuck in ankle-deep wet cement. He heard Ms. Merriweather's voice. It seemed to be coming from inside his own head.

A future so bitter
or another that's sweet.
History lies open
to learn or repeat.
Dreams of kings
are dreamed by pawns.
What could be so right,
for the thoughtless goes wrong.

CHAPTER NINE

Finius's Revenge

After the Dupas had paid their nickels and had been pulled through Sidney, they found themselves somersaulting through space. Faster and faster. They heard the sound of laughter and giggles. Then an unseen woman spoke these words:

> Rambling . . . bambling
> feathers and snouts.
> Oh, yes, dear Dupas,
> here's what you're about.
> Flying through star fields,

traveling so far.
It's time you know
who you really are.

The Dupas fell onto solid ground, but it was like no ground they had ever seen before. The earth was purple. The sky was green. The trees were bright blue. Even though it was daytime, stars twinkled in the sky and two orange moons loomed large on the horizon. The Dupas got up and brushed off the purple dirt.

"I feel weird," Tiny said as he shook himself off.

"You look weird, too," Scarlet replied, and started to laugh. The laughter sounded a little like the caw of a bird.

Tiny was indeed starting to look rather strange. His nose flattened out, and his ears popped up and turned pink. A curly tail tore through the back of his pants, and his hands and feet turned into hooves.

"You pig!" Scarlet chortled.

"That's not very oink." Tiny rubbed his bulging belly. "Why did I say that?" Tiny got down on all fours and looked up at Scarlet. She was laughing hysterically . . . and flapping her wings. "Look at you." Tiny grunted. "I always knew you were one

97

odd bird ... but this?" Tiny rolled around in the purple mud, oinking and oinking for all he was worth.

Scarlet meanwhile had stopped laughing. She was looking down at herself. "Awkk!" she screeched. Her body was covered with very dark brown feathers. A ring of white feathers circled her neck. Her nose had been replaced by a large hooked beak. Her feet were talons, her arms were wings. And her head looked completely bald. Scarlet was a vulture. And vultures do not take kindly to being laughed at by pigs.

"Stop laughing, pork-face," Scarlet warned. "I'd rather be a bird than a side of bacon." Scarlet started licking her beak.

"Okay ... Okay ... Oink-kay." Tiny pulled himself up on his four hooves. "Sorry, birdbrain." Tiny started his oink-and-roll routine once more.

"Tiny, darling ... " Scarlet looked hungrily at her hubby. "Could you please do me a favor and come over here for a moment?"

"Sure, Vultura." Tiny got up and started walking toward Scarlet, his belly rubbing on the ground. "What do you want?"

Scarlet stared at Tiny. She had a strange look in her eye. She answered his question: "Pork chops!"

While Jerry and the rest of the kids were opening doors and listening to Ms. Merriweather, Jerry's dad was finally waking up from his morning nap. He woke up smiling, having dreamed that he was the ruler of Disney World and that he had changed the name of the amusement park to Finius World.

In the dream Mickey, Minnie, Donald, Pluto, and Goofy had objected to the name change. Finius had fired them all. Nothing made Finius happier than a good group firing. "Boy, that felt great," he said, stretching his arms out above his head. But his smile quickly faded.

"I wonder how those two Dupas are doing," he wondered out loud. (Finius said a lot of things out loud when he was alone. He loved hearing his own voice.) The more he thought about the Dupas, the more nervous he became. How could he have been so stupid as to count on the Dupas to get the dirt on that teacher? "Those two animals can't do anything right."

So even though it was almost time for his next

nap, Finius jumped from his chair and rushed to his car. His destination? Marbledale School.

It didn't take him long to get there. He screeched his car into the school driveway and roared into the parking space marked "Reserved—Principal." Finius pulled a cardboard sign that said "Visiting Principal" out of the glove compartment and put it under the windshield.

Finius had a lot of signs—he wanted to be sure he always got the best parking space. He had signs marked "Handicapped," "Doctor," "Diplomat," and "Judge." His favorites were "Prosecutor," "Press," and "President." He particularly liked "President."

Once he had borrowed a friend's car and parked it in the middle of the expressway. Luckily Finius had remembered to bring along his sign that simply read "Abandoned." The friend wasn't as lucky. She never saw her car again.

Finius opened the door and leapt from his car. His plaid sport coat caught in the door when he slammed it shut. It tore neatly up the middle when he ran from the car at full speed. He made a mental note to sue his tailor, then scampered into the school building, heading directly for Room 104.

*   *   *

Meanwhile Ms. Franklin had arrived at her apartment, which was only about a mile and a half from school. She had completely forgotten about the ice pack and bandage. Memories lapped at the corners of her mind . . . there, but just out of reach. Memories that would, once and for all, solve the mystery of Ms. Merriweather.

Ms. Franklin went into her hall closet and started tossing things out behind her. Boots came flying, followed by an umbrella, a folding chair, and a bag full of scarves and mittens. "It's got to be in here somewhere." Ms. Franklin panted as she pushed out a pile of weights, which she had promised she would start lifting, but never did.

Finally in the back corner, under a sack filled with old stuffed animals, Ms. Franklin found what she was looking for. It was a box labeled "School Yearbooks." She ripped it open and frantically searched for the one she had marked "Sixth Grade."

By the time Finius got to Room 104, he was furious. He was sure the Dupas had blown it. With every step he took, his anger grew. He slammed his hand into a locker. "Ouch!" Finius screamed. He made a mental note to sue the locker manufacturer.

The fact that he'd seen neither hide nor hair of the Dupas made his eyes squint, his teeth clench, and his nostrils flare. He was not beautiful when he was angry. "I bet those Dupas haven't gotten one rotten, lousy little bit of underhanded information on that Ms. Quarryceather. And they call themselves teachers? HA!"

So when Finius got to Room 104, he was not in the best of moods—to put it mildly. A little smile came to his lips when he reached the door. "This time, Ms. Larrypeather, you're dealing with a pro."

Finius pulled a stethoscope out of his back pocket. "Let's just give a listen to what's going on in there." He put the stethoscope up to the door. At first he heard nothing. He was about to give up when he detected a very faint sound. It sounded like a small drum a great distance away. As he listened, the beats grew louder.

"Boom-boom." What Finius heard was unmistakably the sound of a heartbeat. He shook his head and pulled the stethoscope from the door. He gave it a quick and violent shake.

"Dippy device must be defective. It still has an old

heartbeat stuck in it. That'll teach me to steal equipment from that dorky doctor brother-in-law of mine."

He put the stethoscope back up to the door. The beating sound was even louder. "Boom-boom. Boom-boom. Boom-boom." Soon the sound was so loud that it actually started to hurt his ears, but he couldn't pull away. Finius could swear the door was starting to pulse in and out with each, ever louder "Boom-boom."

Some fifth-graders walked by in the hall. They acted as if nothing out of the ordinary was going on. Finius couldn't believe it. "Can't you hear it?" he yelled at the kids. "Look at the door. It's beating . . . like a heart."

The fifth-graders had seen plenty of classroom doors before. This one looked like all the rest. But they had never seen a man holding a stethoscope up to one. They decided to be early for their next class and ran down the hall.

"Lousy rug-rodents," Finius squeaked. He kept listening.

"Boom-boom. Boom-boom." The beats kept getting louder and louder. The door was pulsing in and out, faster and faster. Louder and louder . . . faster and faster. Suddenly there was was a crackling sound. Finius saw the wood start to split. Then the entire door exploded.

Now Finius was flying backward through the air. He landed against some lockers. Finius figured he must have blacked out, because the next thing he knew, a first-grader was kneeling next to him. "Are you okay, mister? Why are you sitting down in the hall? You get in trouble?"

Finius stumbled to his feet. "Didn't you hear the explosion?"

"What splosion?" The first-grader looked confused.

"What splosion?" Finius screamed. "The splosion in that room!" Finius pointed at Room 104. He froze midscream. The door was perfectly intact.

"Sure I heard it," the boy said as he backed away. "I heard whatever you say I heard." The boy turned and ran.

Finius didn't even notice him leave. He just stared at the door. He felt his heart beating a mile a minute, pulsing in and out against his shirt. Boom-boom. Boom-boom. Boom-boom. He shivered. Finius searched for some logical explanation for the "splosion" that he saw, but that apparently never happened. "Must have been something I ate. No more refried beans and caramel apples for breakfast."

Finius started to walk toward the door, but stopped. There was a pain in his right foot. He looked down and saw a three-inch piece of splintered wood sticking out from the toe of his shoe. The wood matched the door to Room 104 perfectly.

Ms. Franklin found her sixth-grade yearbook near the bottom of the box. She sat back against her closet wall and started quickly flipping through the pages, looking for her class picture.

Finius yanked the wood out of his shoe and tossed it aside. He was sticking to his indigestion explanation for what had, or hadn't, happened. Indigestion was something he could understand—Jerry and his mom could certainly vouch for that.

Finius put all other possibilities out of his mind. He touched the doorknob that would open the way into Room 104.

I'll just march in there and accuse that old Ms. Jerrycheather of something, he thought. Maybe of teaching with an expired license . . . or speed reading. Something to boot her booty out of here in a hurry.

"Aha!" he screamed as he threw open the door to Room 104. "Aha," he almost whispered when he noticed the room was empty. Not a student, a teacher, or a Dupa in sight. Now Finius was angrier than ever. "How dare that Ms. Scareytether not be here?" Finius stormed across the room. "I expect respect from the people I'm about to fire."

Finius started knocking over desks. He tore posters off the walls and shattered the crystal globe with a yardstick. "Piñata time!" he screamed as the crystal shards fell to the floor. He pulled all the drawers out of Ms. Merriweather's desk and did a tap dance on the papers that fell out.

"Turn my boy's hair blue, will you?" he snorted as he ripped up a notepad. That was when Finius spotted Sidney, standing wide open. "You're next," Finius growled. He ran to Sidney and tried to slam the door shut. It wouldn't move. Finius panted as he pushed against it. "What the jalapeño is she doing with a door in her room?"

Finius gave up on closing Sidney. Instead he tried to knock the whole door over, frame and all. He was like a flea trying to move a block of granite. The door

106

was not about to budge. "Okay. No more Mr. Nice Finius. Time to get my supplies."

"I wouldn't do that if I were you," a voice warned from behind Finius.

"Well, you're not me," Finius yelled as he ran out of the room, heading for his car.

About halfway down the hall he paused. "Who said that?" Finius wondered out loud. Then he shrugged his shoulders, blamed it on indigestion, and ran full speed into the parking lot.

It was easy for Finius to spot his car. It was the only one with a torn plaid sport coat hanging from the door. He ran to the trunk, accidentally smacking himself on the chin when he opened it. Finius hoped there would be a bruise, thinking it would help in the lawsuit he now planned to file against the car-maker. He reached into the trunk and pulled out a big, heavy box labeled "Emergency Supplies. Caution: May be dangerous to children and other living things."

"This oughta slam the door on that turnip of a teacher." Finius giggled with glee. He picked up the box and lugged it up to Room 104.

Apparently Finius wasn't aware that it's wise to put your hands under a heavy box when you're carrying it. As soon as he entered the classroom, the bottom fell out.

His favorite sledgehammer bounced off the big toe on his right foot. A blowtorch slammed into his left foot. Finius screamed and tried to lift and grab both feet at the same time, sending himself crashing to the floor amid a wide array of saws, drills, chains, firecrackers, spray paint, knives, nails, swords, and axes—and two dented cans of brussels sprouts in a light cream sauce. He'd once figured if he ever got really mad at someone, and nothing else worked, he'd make the person eat the brussels sprouts.

"Butterfingers." Finius heard a teasing voice. It came from the direction of Sidney. That's the direction he headed in, sledgehammer in hand. Finius was growling. The door seemed to quake on its hinges.

Finius heard a sarcastic voice say, "Not the hammer. Oh, please, Finius . . . not the hammer. Don't hit me. Don't hit me. Oh! Oh! Oh! Oh! Oh! Finius, you're such a brute."

Without a word Finius slammed the hammer into Sidney. It landed with an enormous bang. For a split second all action came to a halt. There they were: the door, the hammer, and the man. Then a giggling sound filled the room. It came from the other side of Sidney. "Ride 'em, cowboy." The voice laughed.

The hammer head, which was still resting against Sidney's frame, started to vibrate. Then the handle started to vibrate. Then Finius started to vibrate. Still holding the hammer straight out in front of him, Finius shook so hard that all the change popped out of his pockets and two gold fillings came loose. When he finally stopped shaking, he looked at the hammer . . . which instantly crumbled into dust.

Finius ran to his scattered implements of destruction. He grabbed a blowtorch. "Let's see if you can take the heat," he said, lighting the torch and directing the flame right on Sidney's doorknob. Finius could have sworn he heard a female voice saying:

Finius . . . Finius . . .
why haven't you learned?
When you play with fire,
you're apt to get burned.

He held the flame to Sidney for ten seconds . . . twenty seconds. Nothing was happening to the door, but Finius was starting to feel a little warm, very warm.

The longer he held the torch in place, the hotter he got. Soon he was perspiring. On second thought, to say he was perspiring is a bit of an understatement. *Sweat* poured down his face. First a few drops, then more. Soon he looked as though he were in a tropical rain forest. His clothes were drenched and dripping.

He got hotter and hotter, but Finius kept the flame to Sidney. In fact, he turned the torch up to make the flame even bigger. That's when smoke started coming out of his pant legs. First there were just a few wisps. Soon it began to billow.

"Didn't anyone ever tell you it's dangerous to smoke?" the voice from the other side of Sidney asked. Finius dropped the torch and ran screaming for the fire extinguisher in the corner of the room. He stuffed the nozzle down his pants and squeezed the lever. Now the only thing running out of his pant legs was foam. The fire was out, but Finius was still steaming.

He picked up two packs of firecrackers and a roll of tape off the floor. He taped a pack to each of Sidney's hinges and lit the fuses. Finius turned away and put his hands over his ears. A moment later he felt something slide into each of the back pockets on his pants. "Uh-oh."

"Have a blast, Finny baby," the voice whispered in his ear. Finius only had time to swallow before the firecrackers started popping. With each "Bing!" "Bang!" and "Boom!" Finius jumped into the air.

"Youch! Yikes! Yow!" Finius howled as the firecrackers turned the back of his trousers to tatters, revealing his boxer shorts, which had the words *The Seat of Power* stenciled across the back. Finius rubbed his bruised behind. One last firecracker exploded. "Yaaaaahhhhhh!"

"Well, I'm glad you got a bang out of that." The voice from Sidney chuckled.

"That's it!" Finius bellowed. "You've had it now!" Finius grabbed a long chain from the floor. He looped and locked one end around Sidney. The other end he tossed through a window into the parking lot. Finius raced from the room and ran to his car. He attached the chain to the trailer hook he had on the back of his car and put his key in the ignition. Now it was Sidney's turn to say, "Uh-oh."

* * *

Ms. Franklin had found what she was looking for. All of her questions had been answered. There'd been a flash flood of memories that had left her dizzy and short of breath. Everything was now remembered. Everything was now clear. She glanced down at the sixth-grade yearbook that rested on the passenger seat of her car. She was heading back to Marbledale School. The speedometer read almost eighty-nine miles per hour.

After Ms. Franklin had found her class picture, she had sat in stunned silence for a few moments before looking at it a second time. Her class had been quite a group, she now recalled—a class that no teacher had wanted to teach, a class that was out of control. But it wasn't her former classmates that Ms. Franklin was looking for. It was the teacher she wanted to see, the teacher who had helped them grow.

When Ms. Franklin looked at the picture of the teacher standing next to the long-ago children, she found herself staring directly into the face of Ms. Merriweather.

Written in purple ink under the picture was the message:

Dear Barbara, until that someday when we meet again.

As soon as she read those words, Ms. Franklin knew she just had to get back to school . . . and fast.

CHAPTER TEN

Ms. Franklin Saves the Day

Finius turned the key and pressed his foot down on the accelerator. "Take this, you wimp," he cackled as he jerked the stick shift into gear. The car jumped forward, snapping all slack out of the chain. The tires started to smoke. While the wheels spun and the engine roared, the car stayed pretty much in place. Sidney was holding his own. So far the tug-of-war was a draw.

Ms. Franklin pulled into the parking lot. She saw Finius rev up his engine, trying to drive away. She saw the chain with one end hooked to the car and the other through the broken window to Room 104. It was pretty obvious what Finius was trying to do.

"Stop!" she screamed, jumping from her car and running toward Finius. She quickly reached the driver's-side window and started pounding on the glass with her fists. "Stop! You don't know what you're doing, Finius! You don't know!"

Finius looked at Ms. Franklin and stuck out his tongue. "Boy, that felt good," he said once his tongue was back in his mouth. He had always wanted to do that to a principal.

"Don't you understand?" Ms. Franklin shouted over the engine's roar. "All the kids, including Jerry, went through Sidney. Destroy Sidney, and those kids will have no way back."

"Power has its price," Finius yelled back, not really listening to what Ms. Franklin was saying. Goopers, I'm good, Finius thought. I'll have to write that down.

Finius was beyond reason or reality. Ms. Franklin kept pounding on the window. Suddenly the car jerked forward an inch . . . then another. "I'm winning!" Finius cheered. "Soon it will be good-bye, Sidney!"

The car lurched forward another inch or two. Ms. Franklin thought she heard a cracking sound coming from the window to Room 104. Finius was like some wild animal. His lips were pressed back against his teeth. He was holding the steering wheel so tightly that his knuckles turned white. He pushed down on the accelerator with all his might. "I'm winning! I'm winning!"

"Winning doesn't mean you've won," Ms. Franklin said as she ran faster than she'd ever run before, straight for Room 104.

A group of fourth-graders was quite impressed. None had ever seen a principal move so fast. "No running in the hall, Ms. Franklin," a girl named Amanda teased. Ms. Franklin didn't hear her— Room 104 was in sight. She raced through the door, closing it behind her.

When she saw Sidney, she knew they were in trouble. Big trouble. She could hear Finius's car engine screaming and tires squealing outside. She saw the chain links on the windowsill. Each time one more link slipped out, there was the sound of wood splintering.

The chain was wrapped around the middle of Sidney, which was bowed out toward the window.

He was holding his ground, but the hold was getting less secure by the second. By the time Ms. Franklin reached him, Sidney was almost bent in the shape of a half-moon.

The car kept pulling. Sidney's nameplate fell to the ground. Pieces of wood began to splinter off, and the doorknob tumbled to the floor and rolled under the desk. The whole classroom seemed to be shaking from the pressure.

Another link of the chain went over the sill and out the window. A large crack appeared in the center of Sidney. Ms. Franklin knew that there wasn't much time left. She tried to lift the chain off, but it was much too tight to move. She tried to pull on the chain, only to see two more links slip out the window. The crack in Sidney widened.

"I'm winning! I know I'm winning! You know I'm winning!" Finius's crazed voice could be heard above the roar.

There had to be some way to break the chain. Ms. Franklin spotted Finius's ax on the floor. She grabbed it and brought it down hard on the chain. Sparks flew . . . but the chain wasn't even scratched.

She picked up a hacksaw from the floor and started sawing away at a link that rested on the windowsill. The link moved from under the saw and out the window. More wood splintered from Sidney. She tried to saw the next link, only to have it to go out the window. The crack in Sidney had grown into a large, ugly gash.

With each link Finius laughed louder and louder. "I win! It's in the bag! It's a sure thing! End of story! End of Sidney! I WIN! IT'S A LOCK!"

"A lock!" Ms. Franklin stopped sawing. She slapped her hand on her forehead. "Why didn't I think of that?"

Ms. Franklin looked over at the combination lock that held the chain around Sidney. "Let there be time," she whispered. She ran for the lock.

Ms. Franklin was thankful that Finius had used a combination lock. She knew full well that he would never be able to remember the combination. Sure enough, when she reached the lock, she found a small piece of paper taped onto the back. It read, "23 left . . . 22 right . . . 21 left."

There was a loud cracking sound. Sidney was starting to come apart. Pieces of wood were flying around the room. Ms. Franklin turned the lock: 23 left, 22 right, 21 left. The lock didn't open. All at once

Sidney, frame and all, was pulled across the floor and pressed against the window.

Finius's car had jolted forward about ten feet. He was laughing hysterically as he put both feet on the accelerator and pushed down. "It won't be long now," he crowed.

Sidney was bent almost in two. His middle part was actually sticking out the window. Ms. Franklin ran to the window. "The wrong combination? How could he have written down the wrong combination?" She reached outside the window and grabbed the lock. 23 left ... 22 right ... 21 left. Again it refused to open. "What else could it be?" she cried. More wood cracked and splintered. Sidney wouldn't last another twenty seconds.

"I'm sorry, kids. I'm sorry, Sidney. I'm sorry, Ms. Merriweather." Ms. Franklin slumped to the floor. Tears streamed down her face. Then the tears stopped. She got up and reached for the lock.

Ms. Franklin had remembered something she'd heard Jerry say to Mitch in the lunchroom on a day his dad had packed his lunch.

When Jerry had unwrapped his sandwich that day, he'd found the bologna on the outside and the bread in the middle. He'd laughed and told Mitch that his dad had trouble even putting his shoes on the right feet, unless they were marked. "He's a great politician," Jerry had said, "but the guy doesn't know his right from his left."

"Thank you, Jerry." Ms. Franklin smiled. She reversed the order on the lock. "Twenty-three *right*." She dialed as quickly as she could. "Twenty-two *left*. Oh, please let this work. Twenty-one *right*." It worked. The lock popped open. The chain released.

Ms. Franklin heard the sound of cheering kids from behind her, but she didn't turn around. She was too busy looking out the window at what was happening in the parking lot below.

When the chain snapped free, Finius's car shot off like a moonbound rocket. Its front tires lifted into the air in a perfect wheelie. Its back tires left a trail of burnt rubber and smoke. The car zoomed through the parking lot and into the playground, which, fortunately, was empty at this time of day.

It streaked directly toward two side-by-side slides. Finius tried to turn the steering wheel, but he was too late. The tires on the right side of the car

120

flew up one slide. The tires on the left did the same on the other. When the car reached the top, the slides ended, but the car kept going . . . straight up into the air. The space shuttle *Finius* was launched. Higher and higher it shot before making a U-turn and starting back down.

Finius flapped his arms like wings, trying to avoid the inevitable crash landing that was now only moments away. The car had flown past the playground, above a subdivision, and was coming down over an expressway.

Faster and faster it fell. Finius was lucky. The car made a perfect four-point landing on the trailer of a moving truck. "Whew! That was close," Finius said in a relieved voice. Then he said "Whew!" again . . . but for a different reason. Finius held his nose and opened the window. Something smelled terrible. He lifted his arm, trying to remember if he had used deodorant that morning. He'd forgotten, all right, but that wasn't it.

He looked down at what the truck was carrying. He saw black banana peels, old diapers, and coffee grounds. He saw spoiled vegetables, eggshells, and tissues. He saw some things he didn't recognize at all.

The truck pulled into the righthand lane. Finius looked over and saw a sign: "City Dump—Next Exit." Finius quickly rolled up the window and banged on the steering wheel. "I'll get you for this, Ms. AiryMether! No one makes a fool of Finius Q. Sands!"

Finius felt an odd tingling sensation on his head. It started at the back of his scalp and worked its way up to his forehead. He grabbed the rearview mirror and stared in horror at his reflection. His hair was now a most lovely shade of royal blue.

"Barbara. Barbara. Earth to Barbara. You simply must start paying more attention in class." Ms. Franklin heard a happy voice behind her. She had been almost hypnotized by the flying Finius show outside the window.

When Ms. Franklin turned around, Ms. Merriweather was sitting calmly at her desk. Their eyes locked. "Happy someday," Ms. Merriweather said. "And thank you."

Ms. Franklin didn't know what to say. "But . . . How? Why? Where?" she stammered.

"Piddle-dee diddle-dee. You worry so much," Ms. Merriweather said. "Some things you just have to accept, my dear. Some things don't really have explanations as we know them." Ms. Merriweather walked up to Ms. Franklin and gave her a hug. "I knew you'd turn out just fine. I knew it from the first time you tried to put gum in my hair. Remember that?"

Ms. Franklin blushed. She remembered. She also remembered that, somehow, the gum had ended up in her own hair. It had taken her mother two hours to get it out. Ms. Franklin started to giggle.

Ms. Merriweather giggled, too. "It's always gum. No matter the class, someone always tries some gummy business on good old Ms. M."

Ms. Franklin thought about what had just happened. "I'm sure the kids are all right, but I'm sorry about the room." Ms. Franklin was still looking deeply into Ms. Merriweather's eyes. "And about Sidney. That Finius made quite a mess. I hope you can fix him."

Ms. Merriweather looked confused. "There's no need to apologize. Everything seems to be in order."

For the first time since she'd turned from the window, Ms. Franklin broke eye contact with Ms. Merriweather and looked at the room. All of the students were at their desks. Their heads were resting on their folded arms. Peaceful, sleeping smiles were on their faces. Jerry was snoring. Finius's tools were gone. The crystal globe floated in the corner. And Sidney stood tall, proud, and unbroken.

Ms. Merriweather nodded her head toward the class. "I think they've been asleep long enough, don't you? It's time for these fine young scholars to get on with the rest of their lives." Ms. Merriweather snapped her fingers twice, clapped two times, and then snapped her fingers twice more. All of the "fine young scholars" lifted their heads and opened their eyes. Some looked shocked, some frightened, some just thankful to be back at their desks in Room 104.

Mitch raised his hand. "Are we really back, Ms. Merriweather?"

"Of course you're back, Mitchell. Where else would you be?"

The kids looked at each other in silence and thought about everything they had seen . . . or possibly dreamed.

"What is today's dream," Ms. Merriweather said, "good or bad, can be tomorrow's reality. I think you all now know that it's up to you . . . each one of you. Think about it." There wasn't a person in Room 104 who wasn't already thinking about it. Thinking very hard. Ms. Merriweather smiled.

Kelly raised her hand. "But was it a dream? Was everything just a dream?"

"Nothing's ever 'just' a dream, Kelly," Ms. Merriweather replied. "As for what just did, or perhaps did not, happen ... you'll have to decide for yourselves. What is real for you may appear to the world as a silly little dream. What is real to the world might be illusion."

All at once everyone heard a loud squawk coming from the other side of Sidney. There was a frantic pounding at the door. "Let me oink of here! Let me oink! She's going to oink me!"

"Oh, dear," Ms. Merriweather said. She walked quickly up to Sidney and opened the door.

Tiny Dupa came oinking through, with Scarlet in hot pursuit. Both had returned to normal. Well, as normal as they ever were.

"Pork chops! Pork chops! Pork chops!" Scarlet shrieked as she chased Tiny into the classroom. Scarlet held her now human hands like claws. As she ran by, Ms. Merriweather plucked one last remaining tail feather from Scarlet Dupa's derriere. "Ouch,"

Scarlet shrieked, racing after Tiny and out into the hall.

Ms. Merriweather carried the feather over to Sidney. She held it out and shook her head. "Getting a bit sloppy, aren't we Sidney, dear?"

"Sorry. I've had a rough day."

"Not to worry." Ms. Merriweather gave Sidney a gentle pat. She tossed the feather through the door. It vanished in a flash of light.

"Wow!" Jerry said.

Everyone looked at him and started to applaud. Jerry's hair was no longer blue.

CHAPTER ELEVEN

Back to the Present

After Tiny and Scarlet had scampered out of the room, Ms. Merriweather turned to the class. "I wonder who taught those two Dupas when they were young. Maybe they never really were young." Ms. Merriweather threw her hands up into the air. "No matter. People like the Dupas usually wind up getting it in the end."

The class listened quietly. "Well, my kidlets," Ms. Merriweather continued. "I think we can agree that this has been quite an eventful day." Mitch, Kelly,

Lissie, Jerry, Ian, and a couple of others slowly raised their hands to ask a question.

Ms. Merriweather looked out at them. "No," she said softly. "Nothing *has* to be. You are now, and for that matter always have been, masters of your own destinies." The hands started going down, the questions answered without ever being asked. Ms. Merriweather looked from student to student. She looked deeply into the eyes of each one before going on to the next. Kelly was the last. Ms. Merriweather gazed intently, winked, and smiled. Kelly smiled back.

"It looks as though my work here is done." Ms. Merriweather brushed her hands together. "I'm afraid it's time for me to be off."

"Don't go!" "No!" "You can't leave us now!" "We need you!" The class erupted in protest against Ms. Merriweather's announcement.

"Pishidy-poshidy." Ms. Merriweather held up her hands for silence. "You have everything you need right here." Ms. Merriweather touched her forehead. "And here." Ms. Merriweather touched her heart. "Soon, very soon, I'll be a memory. Then I'll be forgotten. That is how it must be."

"We'll never forget!" "No, we won't!" "How could we forget?"

Ms. Merriweather looked directly at Ms. Franklin. "You will forget. You must forget, if you are to be free to choose."

"Will we ever see you again?" Kelly asked.

" 'Ever' is a long time, Kelly. And occasionally 'someday' really does come. Right, Ms. Franklin?"

Ms. Franklin simply nodded her head. When she did, one tear slid down her right cheek. Everyone in the class was fighting back tears, including Jerry.

Ms. Merriweather wiped away a tear from Lissie's cheek. "Now, now, now. This is not the time for tears. You should all be quite pleased with yourselves, for you now have the ability to think. I want smiles," Ms. Merriweather said. "Smiles," she repeated. Ms. Merriweather walked up to Jerry and moved in very close. Their faces were only inches apart. Ms. Merriweather smiled. She didn't move. She stayed nose to nose with Jerry, smiling. Sure enough, not twenty-three seconds had passed before Jerry started to smile, too. He couldn't help it.

"That's better," Ms. Merriweather said before moving on to Mitch. He smiled before she even got to him. "Much better," Ms. Merriweather said. Now everyone was smiling.

Ms. Merriweather turned to Ms. Franklin. "Barbara, my dear, would you do me one more favor?"

"Of course, Ms. Merriweather, anything."

Ms. Merriweather pulled a camera out of one of her vest pockets. "Would you please take a class picture?"

The class lined up, tallest in the back, smallest in the front. Ms. Merriweather took up a position to the right of the front row.

Ms. Franklin focused the camera. "Okay, now . . . watch the birdie." Mitch and Lissie could have sworn that they saw a tiny bluebird flying over Ms. Franklin's head. Some others said they saw a robin. Kelly saw a hummingbird. In any event, the feathered friends vanished as soon as the flash went off.

"Perfect," Ms. Franklin declared.

Ms. Merriweather took the camera and placed it back into her vest pocket. She pulled out a roll of film. "Barbara, would you mind having this developed? I have a feeling the picture will look great in the yearbook."

Ms. Franklin took the film and nodded her head.

Ms. Merriweather walked up to Sidney and

turned back to the class. "What is it they say in Hollywood? Ah, yes . . . I guess that's 'a wrap.' " She looked slowly from student to student. "Now close your eyes, my children. And always remember, never forget to think . . . and to dream."

Even though some tried not to, all of the sixth-graders in Room 104 slowly closed their eyes. A second later, when they opened them, Ms. Merriweather was gone. The room was once again as it had been.

Sidney, the crystal globe, the *Enterprise*, the posters—everything had disappeared. As if none of it had ever really been there at all. The kids sat at their old brown desks. The mural and the teacherometer were nowhere to be seen.

Already the memory of Ms. Merriweather had started to fade. Kelly could still see her in her mind, but the picture was far from clear. Mitch remembered having the strangest dream about spending decades in the sixth-grade. Lissie and Jerry knew something had happened, but they weren't sure what. A moment later the bell rang, and everyone slowly filed out of the room and headed home. In a way they were all looking forward to coming back to school the next day. Mitch was the last to leave the classroom. On his way out he walked up to Ms. Franklin and shook her hand.

The principal stood alone in Room 104 for several minutes after Mitch left. She slowly looked around. She still remembered everything. She hadn't closed her eyes. "Thank you, Ms. Merriweather," she whispered. "From all of us." Ms. Franklin glanced over at the blackboard. In purple chalk she saw the reply: "You're welcome."

Epilogue:

Twenty Years Later

"**T**hey're monsters! Awful, rotten, creepy little monsters! I quit! Quit! Quit! Quit! Quit! Quit! Quit! Quit!" With that, Ms. Prandis ran from Room 201 at Hillscreek School. She pushed through the nearest exit door and rushed for her car.

Ms. Kelly Wockler, the principal, happened to be in the hall at the time. She didn't try to stop Ms. Prandis. She knew there was no point to it. No teacher had lasted more than a week in Room 201. Some had lasted only a few hours.

As she slowly walked back to the principal's of-

133

fice, Ms. Wockler kept repeating: "What do I do now?" When she reached her office, only one word kept going through her mind: "HELP!"

Ms. Wockler paused at the school secretary's desk. "Any calls?" she asked.

"No calls, but there is someone waiting in your office to see you." The secretary handed Ms. Wockler a business card.

Rebecca Merriweather—Teacher

ABOUT THE AUTHOR

JERRY PIASECKI is the creative director for a Michigan advertising agency. Previously he was a radio newsperson in Detroit and New York. He has also written, directed, and acted in numerous commercials, industrial films, and documentaries. The writing he loves most, though, is for young readers, "where one is free to let the mind soar beyond grown-up barriers and defenses." Jerry lives in Farmington Hills, Michigan. He has a thirteen-year-old daughter Amanda, who has a dog named Rusty and a cat named Pepper.